Praise for *Greg Maxwell's Inferno*

"The funniest piece of fiction I've read since Trump's 'The Art of the Deal.'"

—**Mike Sacks,** *author of Stinker Lets Loose, Randy!, Poking a Dead Frog*

"A good novel ought to knock a reader out of their own head and into the thoughts of an individual much different from themselves, and *Greg Maxwell's Inferno* does just that, sending one headlong into the mind of a truly — but hilariously — deplorable individual as he somehow nonchalantly experiences some of the most impossible, imaginative, and consequential sequences ever attempted in a comic novel. What a devilishly fun book is this."

—**Brian Boone,** *contributor, Vulture; author of Great Men of Science, and So You Want to Be an Old Person: Everything to Know for the Newly Old, Retiring, Elderly, or Considering*

GREG MAXWELL'S

Inferno

BY KEITH JAMES

HUMORIST
BOOKS

New York

First Printing: 2021

ISBN 978-1-954158-08-5

Humorist Books is an imprint of *Weekly Humorist* owned and operated by Humorist Media LLC.

Weekly Humorist is a weekly humor publication, subscribe online at weeklyhumorist.com

110 Wall Street New York, NY 10005

weeklyhumorist.com - humoristbooks.com - humoristmedia.com

For Marley and Daisy

One

It is night. I am lying on my Tempur-Pedic bed. My wife, Debra—who is a hateful and nasty person—is asleep next to me. I am supposed to be asleep, but I am not.

I'm a light sleeper. I have kids. Kids like to break stuff when they are young. When they get older, they start pulling on their genitals. They are learning about their bodies, and I think it's terrible. We never did that when I was a kid. We played team-based sports. A group of guys coming together three nights a week to achieve a common goal—that's living. Kids today, they sit on their gaming chairs in a damp room and pull their wieners to something they saw on the Internet. To them, that's an evening. Whatever. Either way, they are making noise, and being a dad means you have to get up and bang on doors until the noises stop. Last time I had a REM cycle was season four of *Friends*. That show would come on, and I'd blackout. Full-blown coma. I love *Friends*. Great show. Everybody likes to say they are one of the characters. I'm none of them. They're awful people.

No. This night I can't sleep because there are noises outside my window. What exactly? I don't know. My blinds are closed, and, you know, I try not to mess with the blinds on my window because I don't know how to close them once I open them. My wife does. The last thing I want to do is allow my wife to help me with something. Then what? I have to say thank you? Get the fuck out of here.

I bite the bullet and open the blinds. I look down at my backyard. It's one rabbit and one coyote, about four feet away from my French drain. French drains are underground, but I know where the French drain is because I installed the French drain. My wife wanted some Israeli landscaper to install the French drain. Ok. Yeah. I'm just going to let some 6'4 tan guy with an exotic accent do manual labor in my backyard in front of my wife and two sons. Sure. What's next? Christmas is canceled and we do Hannukah at his house because he's my dad and is married to my wife and my sons are now my brothers? No. I installed the French drain. Terrible couple days. I ended up doing it wrong and the Israeli guy had to come out and fix it, but he said I was close.

But the rabbit and coyote: they're going back and forth with each other. Nothing physical. It's more like a heated conversation. I tell them to shut up. They look up at me, and they give me a look like, "Okay, we'll take it easy," but I know they're lying. I don't care if it's two different, non-human species. I know the mannerisms of two people who want to continue arguing.

I close the blinds and try to get a good hamstring stretch in, but yeah, sure enough, they're screaming again. I open the window this time so the rabbit and coyote can hear me real good. My wife is like, "Greg, go back to bed. Don't engage with animals. They can't understand you, and you can't understand them." I'm like, "You haven't talked to me in four days, and this is what you say to me? Put your goddamn sleep mask back on and roll over."

I scream at these two knuckleheads, "Either do it or don't!" I recently got my son to YouTube me some clips from *The Wire*. There is a guy—black guy—Marlo, who said this on the show. He was referring to his friend murdering, or not murdering, a crackhead who scratched his car. In the case of the rabbit and coyote, I don't know what "it" is. I just wanted them to shut up. I've only watched clips of *The Wire*—full show is too confusing (it's no *NCIS: New Orleans*)—but I would definitely be Marlo.

The coyote looks confused. The rabbit is not confused at all. The rabbit is aware that it is go time. He nods at me, then goes at the coyote. The coyote was not prepared for this direct action. Some people are just talkers. It seems like the coyote is a talker. Gun to my head, I would say that I am also a talker. I would never admit this in public, but any type of confrontation—healthy or not—is a real fear of mine. I also can't take criticism. But with all that said, I would definitely consider myself a tough guy you should not mess with.

But yeah, the rabbit gets its paws on the coyote. The coyote can't really get a good defense up, and the rabbit manages to work its paws inside the coyote's mouth. So he's got the coyote's jaws in each paw. The rabbit lifts the coyote over his head. This is an insane amount of core strength, and it clearly is testing the rabbit's core. The rabbit is breathing hard. Undisciplined breathing. I want to tell the rabbit that breath control will add reps but people get weird about workout advice. But, okay, the rabbit has the coyote up over his head by its jaws. Then—I shit you not—he tears the coyote in half. Huge mess. Blood all over my back patio. My wife has all these goddamn wind chimes she blew up our credit cards for, and those are covered in blood. Not going to get a good chime anymore. There you go again, Debra.

The rabbit is soaked. He's all fired up on his murder. As he should be. His actions have fucked up my night, but if I'm over here criticizing his performance, then I've got a real brain or attitude problem. The rabbit paces around for a bit to catch its breath. The rabbit stops moving. Its little rabbit chest slows its heaving down.

The rabbit looks up at me. He stares at me. He raises his paw and points a little paw finger at me. I look at him like, "So what?" My sprinklers go off. The rabbit runs away. Gone.

I head downstairs because I have to deal with this shit before morning. I am almost sure it would not be good for my kids to see a gruesomely murdered coyote. But I don't know. My youngest son Ethan is nine. He's soft. He spends all weekend blowing bubbles and picking flowers for his mother. I think a dead body would be good for him to see, but not this one. This one is a little much. It's insane. This dead body is insane. Too insane. The dead body he needs to see is one he can get a paragraph out of in a college essay. The right dead body makes a reach school a target school. Don't get mad. It's true. You can't get mad if it's true.

My older son, Danny, is sixteen. He's on his computer beating his dick and making his room smell like a salami factory. His whole room is beyond damp. It is moist. I have no concept of what he likes or dislikes. I know he loves masturbating. The young man likes to beat his dick. Sometimes I'll take him to the mall and point at things to gauge his reaction to whatever I pointed at. I'll point at people his age and ask if they are his friends. Nothing. I'll point at a store and ask if it is in his top ten of favorite stores. Nothing. A part of me wants to leave the coyote, wake Danny up, and show it to him. I want to watch him experience something. Then I can ask him, "Hey, this murdered animal: is this good or bad?" If he says "good," ok. That's an issue. If he says "bad," great: my son is a regular guy.

If he says, "I don't know" or "I don't care," it will crush me.

I decide to clean up the coyote. I grab four paper towels and a trash bag and I do my best. I know I have Windex, but I can't find it, so I do a dry rub. I go up the stairs and back to my bedroom. I crawl under the covers and fart on my ungrateful wife. I fall asleep.

Two

I am up at 5AM. Morning workout is mandatory. I have gym clothes sitting by my bed. They're not really clothes. It's a full-body sauna suit. So it's like a fancy garbage bag. Very dangerous, but alarmingly fast results. I put it on quickly. If I don't have the sauna suit by my bed, I won't go to the gym because then I have to fuck around in the dark to find the sauna suit. If I turn on the lights, my wife will act like I shot her, and I'm not trying to have a conversation with my wife in the morning.

I like a protein shake before the gym. Protein powder. Whole Milk. Peanut Butter. Ice Cream. Strawberries. Handful of chocolate chips. I put it in the blender. Everyone hates when I turn on the blender. But if they hate it so much, they should say it to my face. Even if they did, I wouldn't be able to hear them because the blender would be on. Ha! That's good stuff.

My protein shake comes out to a little more than a pint. I read in a chatroom that you should drink it fast, so I drink it fast. I always feel terrible, but that's just how it is.

I am out the front door. I make it five steps before I vomit on the dragon fruit my wife insists on growing. I don't want to speculate, but I think it's the protein shake that made me throw up. The sheer power of my vomit knocks my car keys out of my hands. What do I drive? Mitsubishi Eclipse. I saw the Eclipse in *Fast and the Furious*. Had to have it. It's standard grey with nothing special because I don't have time to be running around finding stickers or slick parts for my car. I'm an adult. I'm not bagging on the characters in *Fast and the Furious*. Cars are their life. Of course they have time for the stickers.

I'm feeling around for my keys. I can't help but notice how hot the ground is. I'm not Johnny-Touch-the-Ground-for-Temperature-Purposes, but I try and touch the ground to see how hot it is at least a couple times a day. I'm only touching the ground at this moment because I'm looking for my keys. It's not one of the scheduled times I touch the ground, but it's worth noting how hot the ground is. I don't make any actual notes on my phone, but I keep a mental note.

I find my keys. I get in the car. I go to the gym.

First thing I do when I go to the gym is have diarrhea in the bathroom. It's been happening ever since I started having protein shakes. I'm in the handicap stall for forty-five to an hour. I like the handicap stall because I need a wide stance to get everything out. They've got good handrail support in case you have to try out some new moves to get your body working. And for all you PC freaks out there: I've been doing this for a long time. I've seen plenty of people in wheelchairs be able to use the normal stalls.

Regardless of the legroom, it is pretty scary stuff. The things that come out take me down a serious WebMD rabbit hole. Whatever. You gotta keep moving. Anxiety increases belly fat. You know where I read that? WebMD.

I don't wipe. Not at 24Hr Fitness. I don't like using the toilet paper at 24Hr Fitness. 24Hr Fitness is real cheap. You are paying to work out. You are not paying to wipe your asshole, and it shows. One-ply at most. And—I should have mentioned this earlier—I have very delicate skin around my butthole. One wipe, and I start to get faint.

I get done with today's diarrhea. Again, very scary. I get naked in the stall. I flush. When I open the stall door, I try to get from the toilet to the showers as fast as possible. I mean, bodies are bodies, but my buttcheeks are profoundly soiled. You want to keep a level of decorum in the locker room. If people see my dirty buttcheeks, it reflects poorly on 24Hr Fitness. I operate in a low-knee sprint to keep my feet close to the floor. I usually lecture strangers on running in a high-knee sprint, but when you are dealing with a wet surface, you are rolling the dice with an ACL tear.

24Hr Fitness gives you two options for showering. You can have a private stall, or you can shower in the community shower. My thought is this: if you shower in a private shower, why don't you towel off with your mother's dress, you small-dick bum? I go community shower, middle faucet, every time. My penis is ok. Really, really thin. But I'm in the community shower, so, who knows, you know?

When I get the water on, my first priority is my butthole. I learned that if you go into a downward dog, you can get all the necessary parts lined up with the stream of water. So, hands on the tile, I pop my butt into the air. The water pressure sends my sensitive balloon knot into deep fissures, but I get a good stretch into my calves and hamstrings. God, honestly, I do not credit this part of my workout enough. Feels great. Sometimes I'll swing my right leg over my left and land into a bridge. The hot water burns the living fuck out of my penis, but I get this lower back stretch that I can't get anywhere else. But today's not a bridge day. I don't know. With the coyote and the protein shake, I feel truly awful.

Turns out, I'm in pretty bad shape. I last four seconds in downward dog, and I pass out.

...

I'm dreaming now pretty meat and potatoes dream about that rabbit the rabbit is speaking English at me about me there are a couple images of Earth and everybody on Earth is holding hands and I'm in the middle and the person to my right has got a really soft hand it's not the rabbit's hand human hand the rabbit is talking but I'm not really listening because the rabbit is kind of annoying other dream stuff happens but I'm more focused on the soft hand I'm not a hand freak but sometimes there's a hand you feel that is so soft it makes you think I dunno that this person really takes care of themselves at some point I lose interest in the soft hand and I tell myself to wrap the dream up.

...

I wake up surrounded by naked men. All showering. I'm lying in my shit, getting no attention. I ask the guy next to me what time it is. He says it's three in the afternoon. Jesus. I was out cold for nine hours. I honestly feel a little better. Maybe I needed sleep. I don't know. I do one of those kung fu snap ups. My form kicks ass, but I broke my own wet surface rule. Come down hard and slap my head on the back of the tile. Hear a pretty good crack inside and outside of my skull. I log roll to a different shower faucet before anyone can trace the head blood back to me. Rock and Roll.

I like to look at everyone's dick when I take a shower. Not for long. Just a peek. Why? Because I want to see what everyone's dick looks like.

There's more to it. I live in a town called Rancho Bernardo. Little north of San Diego. Nice. A lot of Mormons. There's a Souplantation and a park, so it's great. I've lived in other places. Some have Souplantations, and some don't. I say all of this to say that being in Rancho Bernardo, I have seen more uncut dicks than anywhere else. It's crazy. Naturally, I started to wonder if it's a Mormon thing. Lots of Mormon guys, lots of uncut dicks. Correlation—but is it causation? I've got a lot of free time, so I ask every Mormon guy in Rancho Bernardo if they are cut or uncut. And this could also be a Mormon thing, but I have not gotten a firm yes or no. My wife tells me to stop talking about it. I'm like, why? It's harmless. And what, I'm not supposed to be curious?

Today is no different. All the dicks are uncut. Community shower so, you know, a bunch of hung monsters. I try to give everyone their space, but I throw a couple head nods. I think head nods are ok. If we lock eyes or someone catches someone else peeking, I think it's good to nod. No one else does it. Boggles my mind. People are walking around all day staring at their phones and computers. This is one of the few places you are encouraged to put your phone away. Why not take that time to connect to other people? I think it is an introvert/extrovert type thing.

Passing out got me no less covered in shit. Now I have to clean it off my whole front side. Just another thing I have to do. Whatever. I get it done. I don't towel off. The water tricks your body into sweating more.

I'm excited to get a good pump going. I know it's 3:30 in the afternoon, but if you can start your day with a hard workout, you're setting yourself up for success.

I use no machines. Complete waste of time. Have you ever done a push-up? Just do push-ups. The best part about push-ups is that you can just keep doing them. You can do 100? Ok. Do 200. You can do 300? Ok. Do 400.

I am stuck at 35. I do seven wide-stance, seven fist push-ups, seven normal-stance; I try to do seven with my hands close together like a diamond, but that never works. I do seven with my feet on a chair, and then whatever's left, I stand up and do push-ups with my hands on the wall.

Can't break 35, though. If I have to be honest, it emotionally cripples me. I have taken every testosterone pill known to man, and I still can't get over the hump. It might be a mental block. I don't know. I see other men at the gym crushing it, and it fills me with sorrow. I hear the banging and screaming of these stronger men, and I know that if they ever wanted to, they could come into my house and physically dominate me. My kids and wife would become their kids and wife. I would be forced to watch them assume my place like some broken animal. But whatever.

For cardio, I do laps along the interior of the gym. People get bent out of shape because I'm running close to the weight racks, but my body knows when it is on a treadmill. I run until I cramp up.

For a cool-down, I sit on the leg press machine and fall asleep. Tight workout. On a regular day, I'm in and out of the gym in three, four hours.

Three

I step outside 24Hr Fitness and into the general strip mall area that defines Rancho Bernardo. Rancho Bernardo is the type of place to live if you feel like San Diego has moved too fast for you. All the buildings are brown. There's a lot of wood. All restaurants serve meat, and we treat young people like shit. Every store is practical. A car store. A bank. We even have a bead store, but it's not one of those hipster "I love beads, but only because it makes me seem like a fucking crazy person." No. This is a bead store for honest, hardworking people who want to throw beads on their clothes. I dunno. It's a great town.

I do a Jamba Juice to get my post-workout protein. I get chocolate, peanut butter, and a little bit of water. They give it to me for free on the grounds that I come into the back of the store so they can watch me eat it. It's three fifteen-year-olds who play on the high school lacrosse team. They are all skinny and sexy and look like little serial killers. Sometimes they call me a fat pig and make oinking sounds, but whatever. If you are not drinking protein after a workout, don't even bother working out. They got me a doggy bed that I can sleep on in case I get sick. Good kids, raised right.

I don't get sick this time. I down my protein pretty quick. One of the kids teaches me this handshake where he slaps me across the face seven times. It feels good to be included. My son Danny doesn't even notice when I walk into a room. Look at me, sniveling. It's already 8PM. I missed work entirely.

I work a blue-collar job as General Manager for the San Diego Padres. It's a punch-in, punch-out gig. Hard hat and lunch pail type of job. People—Major League Baseball, ESPN, etc.—try to tell me, "Greg, it's not a punch-in, punch-out job. It's one of the highest executive roles in a baseball organization. You are in charge of the Padres' competitive strategy. Stop bringing a construction helmet to work." And I'm like, "Relax." Drives them crazy. But what else am I going to do? Sit with a pencil and watch a baseball game four nights a week? Take notes? Come on. Regular people go to one, maybe two games a year. And—to be clear, these are my words and not Major League Baseball's—I'm just a regular guy. I pretty much use the job to rack up miles so I can party with my friends, also known as "The Boys." I don't know if I'm ready to open up about The Boys, but just know that they are my lifeblood, and I would fucking die for most of them!

The Padres are a lousy team. And I don't know much about baseball, so I'm no help. Didn't play as a kid. But I'm like most guys, where I can see a person doing something, and, even if I don't know what they are doing or I've never done it before, I can explain to them how it should be done. I want to do that with the Padres, but I'm sorry the game is too boring. I saw this one game where the right fielder didn't move once. Ball never came to him. And when he was up to bat, he struck out twice. This guy put on a full baseball uniform, stood around for four hours, and people paid money to watch him do that. Unbelievable.

Watching this guy kind of shaped my GM philosophy. I don't know who is good or bad at this stupid game, but I know what not doing anything looks like. And me personally? As the GM of the San Diego Padres? I want guys who do stuff. So, no, we don't have a right fielder. Everybody in the outfield has to spread out. The catcher is also gone. There is an umpire back there. When the pitcher throws the ball, the umpire can go get it and throw it back. And if there happens to be some dramatic play at the plate and we don't have a catcher to make the tag, then, okay, sue me. I tell the reporters who cover the team this and they freak out. Jesus. Get a life.

Four

I leave Jamba Juice. Man, beautiful night. The moon is full. Big, juicy looking moon. Really giving this strip mall parking lot the business. I find the Big Dipper pretty quickly. Good stuff. A few years back, I had this week where I was big on stars. Got a book. Didn't read it. But I'd sit outside and drink beers with my friends and look up at the sky. Good week.

I can tell I got a good workout because the rubber on my shoes is melting. I don't know what the steam from the pavement is all about, but the rubber on my shoes melting has to be from the workout. Sometimes, I don't know, you really get a good pump in. Can't dwell on it, though. You have to wake up and do it again. I look at the blue paint on a handicap space bubbling like water in a pot. I fart and spit. My spit makes a pretty distinct crackling noise when it hits the pavement. I choose to not process that information, and I smell my fart instead. Horrendous. I need a probiotic. Something is wrong.

My car is the only car in the parking lot. All the streetlights are off. No people. I turn around to the Jamba Juice, and it is empty. The sign lights are turned off. Those lacrosse kids move fast.

In fact, all the sign lights of every shop are turned off. The only light I see is from the moon. There must be a game on.

I turn back around to face my car. A little bit of pavement steam clears, and fifty feet from my car, I see ten people in a perfect circle.

Right away, I look for a hacky sack. If there is a hacky sack, I'll join the circle. I'll hacky sack with anyone for five minutes.

I see no hacky sack, so I'm like, great, ten adults in a complete circle and no hacky sack: must be some stupid improv comedy thing. None of them are fat and bald, so it must be a new team. They all have the same hooded, blood-red robe on. They are chanting a bunch of nonsense and making stupid hand gestures, and that pretty much confirms this is some dumb improv comedy thing. And you know, it really upsets me. Like, you need all of the parking lot to do your goofy shit? You can't be ashamed and do this in private? I try not to make eye contact because if you make eye contact, then they're gonna want you to sign up for classes. Now I'm shelling out $400, so some strangers can hug me once a week.

There are a lot of dead animals in the circle. Mostly rabbits, one field mouse, and gun to my head, I would say two yellow-bellied marmots. Comedy is weird these days. You know what I like to do to get a laugh? I have my son YouTube me a "Who's on First?" I only need to watch half of it, and I got all the comedy I need for a couple of days.

But you know, this improv team has got a lot of dead animals, and they're chanting, and the inside of the circle is starting to glow orange so, I dunno. I watch a little bit.

They start chanting my name "Greg Maxwell. Greg Maxwell. Greg Maxwell." Not a big deal. Happens a lot. I usually leave my driver's license on my windshield, so I know which car is mine.

I call out to them, "Give me my license back and study real performance art!" They all hiss. Improv people are the worst.

They take off their hoods. Okay. Potentially bad news: every person in the circle isn't a human. Primarily coyotes all on their hind legs. Couple bobcats. If I said bonobo, I would be wrong, but I don't know what else it could be, so I'll say bonobo.

The hissing and chanting gets louder. It actually gets pretty annoying. I try and tell them to stop, but they can't hear me. I dig in my pocket for my phone so I can take a picture of the bonobo, and my wallet falls out. The wallet unfolds. My license is in my wallet. Huh. I feel stupid even thinking this, but maybe they know me from the zoo or something?

The hissing and chanting turn into a loud scream that lasts for a while. Right when I think they are going to need a breath, the inside of the circle explodes, and a giant tower shoots out of the hole. Real big tower. It's kind of like the Leaning Tower of Pisa, but it's all black and weeping blood. The ten hooded animals are engulfed in flames, and I can hear them screaming for joy as they are burned alive.

Everything stops. Tower stays put. The animals are ash. I'm eyeballing this tower. I'm thinking 660, 670 feet high? The parking lot is ruined. My car has a scratch on it, but I think the scratch was when Ethan held baton practice in our garage.

Now the sky does this thing where it stops being nighttime. Let me try to explain. You know a sunset? Take out all the parts that are not red. Now make everything red. Make the red the color of blood. There you go.

The tip of the tower swells up fast. It's getting riled up. It's gotta burst, and it does. The tower shoots a big rope of hot, black blood, and following that rope are, gosh, a hundred thousand winged creatures? They're not doing anything crazy, just moving in a circular pattern around the tower, but I wouldn't take my eye off them. I mean, I do take my eye off them because I have other stuff to do with my life, but I'm just saying.

A little black cloud forms at the top of the tower. The cloud gets superthick. Big, thick cloud. I can't see the top of the cloud, but I'm thinking, *I bet you could walk on that cloud it's so goddamn thick.*

The cloud starts to come down the tower. There is something standing on top of the cloud. A thing, something, I don't know. It's not a bonobo.

As the cloud gets closer to the ground, I am able to see what is standing on the cloud. It's like a hoofed beast. Not a centaur. Two legs. This thing looks kind of weak in the calves, but man, its thighs are bananas. Big spiral horns on his head. If you're thinking of a standard mountain ram's horns, you would be wrong, but you would be close.

He is big. I say "he" because I'm looking at his massive penis and balls. I get it: he may be something else, but I'm not going over to the demon guy riding on a cloud asking him what he wants to be called. I'm having a busy day.

His dick is cut. Interesting. Perfectly circumcised. Nothing blocking the tip but a little skin left over to keep the thickness. Really professional stuff.

This guy is holding a fancy stick with one hand and his free hand is pointing at me. I'm getting pointed at a lot. I'm noticing that, and I'm not liking that. I'm like, *fuck off. Who are you?*

He responds, but the place where I think his mouth is, is not moving. He is responding inside my head, "I am the champion sent by Lucifer to claim the mortal realm for Eternal Damnation."

Okay. So this guy is a thought-reader. If he wants me to be impressed, I'm not. You know who was a thought-reader? Mel Gibson in *What Women Want*. You want to share a talent with Mel Gibson? Let's see how that goes over.

I respond back inside my head. *First off, watch your mouth. Cover your dick. Don't be an animal. Second, I don't know who you thought you were pointing at, but I am a homeowner. I own land on this mortal realm, and I don't plan on selling until one, maybe two of my sons go to college. So, if you want to claim any part of the mortal realm that I own, you will need to make a truly outstanding offer. Last, your tower looks like shit. It looks bad. You want to claim other people's things, but you can't even take care of the things you already have. You need gutters. You probably need other stuff, but I can tell you right now that a gutter system would knock out eighty percent of the bullshit I am seeing.*

Unprovoked, he starts up again. "At my order, my army will murder every man on Earth, leaving only women and children to bed and enslave."

I'm like, *calm down. Don't be disgusting. Why is your stupid tower here?*

He says, "This, Greg Maxwell, is your labyrinth. Scale my tower. Defeat the nightmares I have built, and I will spare this mortal realm the pain of war. If you reach the top of the tower, Earth's fate will be decided by combat between you and me."

When you and I fight, is there a point system? Are body punches equal to head punches? I gotta ask these questions because I know guys like him wouldn't volunteer point system information. I wouldn't.

"It is a fight to the death, Greg Maxwell. And when your body expires, I will spread your blood across the Earth, sealing the world's fate and fealty to Lucifer, Belial, Angel of the Abyss, and God of This Age!"

Okay, so there is a point system. I pull out my phone. First, I make sure that I saved that bonobo photo somewhere I can find it. Second, I open up my calendar app. I feel the cloud guy looking at me, so I let him know that I'm checking on something.

Nothing major. Few meetings I can skip. Someone on Facebook has a birthday, but I don't know what I am supposed to do about that. I put my phone away.

Fine, I say inside my head. *I'll do tower stuff. I'll fight you. But I'm gonna go home and fuck around for a little bit. I'll be back in two, three hours.*

He's like, "No, you can't do that."

I'm like, *you got a rule book on that cloud, you stupid fuck? Get out of here.*

He comes back with, "If you leave this tar field—" and I interrupt him.

It's called a parking lot. You want this mortal realm? Maybe know what a parking lot is. You had your tower land in America. You're gonna see a lot of parking lots, and if you call them "tar fields" you're gonna confuse people.

Now he's screaming in my head. "LEAVE THIS PARKING LOT, AND I WILL BEGIN EARTH'S DESTRUCTION."

I'm like *okay, asshole. You're not going to destroy Earth because you want Earth. If you wanted to destroy Earth you would have done it. But what did you do? You had your tower cum out some flying people, and you made a cloud. If you want to threaten me with more clouds, knock yourself out. I'll be back in two hours. I just want to go home and sit down for four seconds. I slipped really bad today and I shit myself. The shit might have gotten into my head wound. I don't know. But I'd like to get some answers and get off my feet before I do tower stuff. Once I sit, check my head wound, do some google searches, I'll come back here, and I'll beat the living shit out of you.*

There's no more talking in my head so the conversation is over. I get in my car and go home.

Five

I didn't directly go home. Honestly, I kind of forgot about that whole Lucifer's champion thing. As soon as I turned the engine, "Night Moves" came on the radio. Bob Seger. Fuck, man! "Night Moves" is about fucking at a drive-in movie theater, and doing it so well that the drive-in movie theater put you on the front page of the newsletter. It's the best song that's ever been made. So "Night Moves" came on, and I forgot what I wanted to do. I drove down to Poway to get donuts from this Thai place. Me and the owner have an incredible back and forth. One time, we were having such a blast, I let him play right field for a Padres game. He made an ass out of me and himself, but we put that behind us. Friends can do that. He's not one of The Boys, though. Has to be said.

So yeah, I'm on my way to a great time at the donut place, but two shit things happen. One, donut place is closed. I forgot it was night. The blood-sky is going to ruin my sleep cycle, and I'm already surly about that. Two, I'm starting to hear my name chanted outside. Loud chant. Loud enough that it is drowning out "Night Moves". I roll down the window to figure out what car is chanting my name so loud. Not a car. All of those flying things are chanting my name. And it's not an encouraging chant.

I have no idea how I am supposed to relax with that chanting. It's a dirty trick. I'm starting to think Lucifer's champion isn't going to play this one straight. I turn off the radio and head back home.

I get home. All my neighbors are outside looking up at the sky. Everyone is hysterical. When they see me, they demand answers. What the fuck do I know? I mean, yeah, I know the situation and the stakes, but I'm not some camp counselor. What, now that I talked to Lucifer's champion, I gotta knock on every door and explain shit to strangers? I just want to get inside my house and sit for a second.

I'm trying to get everyone to understand that this is not my fault and it's probably their fault, or that this doesn't actually exist, and they are being irrational, but it's a tough thing to do to a large crowd of people with tangible evidence. There is a lot more screaming, mainly at me.

Someone calls my name. "Greg Maxwell." It's a soft voice. I follow the sound. It's low. In the grass.

I trace the sound to a rabbit. The rabbit is surrounded by two other rabbits and a gopher. The rabbit in front waves at me. I check the back of my head where I fell on the ground. It's bleeding, but not too bad. No brain fluid, so this is all real.

I recognize the main rabbit. He tore that coyote in half. Crazy shit. Now he is wearing a tunic. Everyone in his group is wearing tunics. They are all made out of baby clothes. His says "Future Feminist." Okay, future feminist rabbit. Give me a break.

I say "Hi."

He says "Hello" back. Conversation kind of stalls. This is my first time having a two-way conversation with an animal. Big stuff, but still kind of boring. Then he's like, "I have two requests. First, I require the corpse of the coyote I battled early this morning. Seco—"

I interrupt him, but quickly apologize. I thought he was done speaking. He starts up again.

"—Second, we have items to discuss before you venture into the tower. It is imperative."

I ask the rabbit who he is. The rabbit smiles. He says his name is unpronounceable. Oh my God. "Do your best," I tell him. He makes a sound, and no shit, it sounds like Doug. "So your name is Doug?" I say. He's like, "I mean, yes, but without an appreciation of my name's ancestral roots, you're missing the full texture of its diction."

I'm calling it now: Doug is a real asshole. I tell Doug to meet me around the back of my house by the trash cans. I'm not talking to animals on my front lawn. I'm not giving that ammunition to my strangers. He says okay, and he and his crew move out.

I get inside my house. Immediately, I am bum-rushed by my family. Well, Ethan and Debra bum-rush me.

"We are scared."

"Where have you been?"

"I can't find my Nintendo Switch charger."

"Hell has cracked the surface of this earth."

Danny says nothing. He's on Google looking at Dave Navarro's tattoos. He seems to have no opinion about what is happening. Come on, Danny. Don't be like this.

I nip all of this in the bud. "Everybody needs to shut up. I'm not here to find Nintendo Switch chargers. I came here to sit down for four minutes, but right now, I have to talk to Doug. Doug is a rabbit. If anyone asks, though, Doug is not a rabbit. I think once everything gets back to normal, I can make some money off talking to animals, but right now, I don't need that kind of heat on me."

The room is quiet. I have some time to look around. Damn. We've been running two different watt bulbs in the kitchen.

"Guys, we've gotta make a decision on what watt bulb we use. Come on."

My wife bursts into tears. Curtains up, Debra. Time for your little show. She starts screaming at me. "You did this! You did this! They are chanting YOUR NAME. We are going to DIE because of YOU."

I do a slow, horizontal karate chop of the air. I put the whole room in timeout. "Debra, have a glass of water." Debra closes her eyes, and all of her shaking pries two fat tears away from her eye lashes.

I say nothing to Ethan. I don't know how this is going to turn out. But I think, either way, this will be good for him. The best thing for Ethan would be to wander the earth Mad Max style. I thought this before any of this tower nonsense. It would help him grow up a little. The comfort of a home has made him soft. Best case scenario, I beat the demon on top of the bleeding tower and Ethan is on his own in a normal world. Worst case scenario, he walks alone in Hell on Earth. Either way, builds character, and he might have a few laughs.

I open the screen door that gets you to the backyard. I turn back to my family and give them a look that says, "not your finest moment".

I finally make it outside. Even though everything looks crazy, it still feels nice. Still San Diego weather. I see Doug and his crew sitting by the trash can. They seem like good people. Real sharp. They pay attention. I feel bad about judging Doug.

Doug doesn't waste time. "The coyote, please." I grab the coyote out of the trash can. He takes it. He gives it to the gopher. I ask why he needs the coyote. "This coyote, like all coyotes, are servants and messengers of Lucifer. I had to intercept this coyote before he could reach you."

"What did the coyote want with me?" I ask. Doug shakes his head. He looks up at the blood-sky. He smiles again, and you know what? I don't like when Doug smiles.

"For all intents and purposes, everything," Doug says. "But, he failed. And paid a price. And we need his body for when the war begins. We don't want to be fighting him twice, do we?"

23

"What war?" I say, but then I remember the war part. "There's not going to be a war. Because I'm gonna go up the tower and kill that guy. He said if I beat him, no war."

No one is making eye contact with me. Doug ends up speaking. "It's delicate, isn't it? The situation we find ourselves in."

"No," I say.

"Greg, are you curious why you are to fight Lucifer's champion?"

"His tower came into the 24HrFitness parking lot. That's where I work out."

Doug smiles again. "Yes, but why you?" I don't really know how to say the last thing I said again. I'm learning a lot about Doug. Doug likes knowing stuff that you don't know. Big power thing. If I didn't see the coyotes do the whole séance, I would assume that Doug and his friends were the bad guys because Doug is such a dickhead.

"Greg, what if I told you that all beings on this earth can be placed on a spectrum of Good and Evil?"

"I don't know. Like, are you asking me if you are *allowed* to tell me that? I mean, you just told me. Is this going well?"

Doug chuckles softly. Fuck Doug. Honestly, I bet Doug is a pervert. I hope part of this journey is that I learn something bad about Doug and I get to expose Doug for who he really is.

Doug climbs up on my trashcan. He does this thing with his paws, and suddenly it's like we are in an IMAX Theater. Everything on the sides of me has gone dark, and I am looking up at some interactive cinematic experience. Doug makes a bunch of people on Earth appear. They are all lined up holding hands and, oh shit, I saw this in a dream.

"Every person plays a role in the balance of morality on this earth. Some, smaller than others. But the collective of us determines the harmony of our universe. Too much good or bad, and we are thrown into chaos. We implode."

Earth blows up. Tasteful special effects. The IMAX Theater effects are solid. Even feel a little air conditioning on the back of my neck. Good on Doug.

Doug's face shows up on the IMAX screen. It is detached from his body, but not in a weird way.

"Would you say then, Greg, that moral balance is important to the preservation of our planet?"

"Yes," I say to Doug's useless question.

"So it's clear that your importance can't be overstated?"

What? "No, it's not clear." Goddamnit. I should have stayed inside.

Doug's face does a slow fade out. I'm back looking at the Earth. I'm flying over the top of every man and creature holding hands in a perfect line. I do a quick cut. I'm still flying over the top of everybody, but I'm clearly coming from another direction. We're doing these two shots back and forth. It's too many cuts. Overproduced. I got the point a few minutes ago, but now it's getting silly.

"As I said earlier, some play larger roles than others. But you, Greg Maxwell, you play the largest role of them all."

The cuts stop. My flying slows over two people. One of those people is me. I start to glow.

"You, Greg Maxwell, are the Dividing Line of Good and Evil."

Doug looks at me with his big smug face.

"Only two people on this earth straddle the sides of Good and Evil with almost perfect individual harmony. Alone, they maintain the balance of this universe. Apart, destruction is inevitable.

It's the reason why Lucifer sent his champion to fight you. If one of you dies, it disrupts the balance of the Earth. It would cause the Earth to crumble."

At this point, he is leaning up against the fence not even looking at me.

"We've kept your identity a secret for years. But the events of last night confirmed who you were."

One of the other rabbits jumps forward, "You shouldn't have taken the night patrol, Doug! It should have been someone else! They knew Greg was Zquartog because you were on patrol. You fell into their trap!"

"BILL—" Doug yells. "—his name is Greg."

"What's the point? They know who he is now."

"Who?" I ask.

"Who knows who you are?" Doug asks.

"Look, I have like, five 'who' questions," I say. Doug shakes his head at Bill. We're still in a little bit of an IMAX world, so maybe there is more Doug wants to show me.

"Is now a good time for questions?" I ask. Doug nods, and the IMAX effects go away. The air conditioner was one of the gophers who crawled up my back and gently blew on my neck. I slap the gopher off me.

"I guess my first question is, what animal do you think this is?" I show Doug the picture of the bonobo. He says it's a bonobo. But he also says it could be something else. Fine.

"Okay, so my next question is, who is keeping me safe, and who is not?"

"Rabbits. Gophers," Doug says.

"Not coyotes."

"Not coyotes."

"Dogs?"

"Dogs are neutral."

"Are coyotes dogs?"

"No."

"Fine," I say. I've entirely lost interest. I'm 100% positive coyotes are dogs, so I think after Doug leaves my trash cans, he should go to a library.

"It's important that you know who is on the side that protects the current state of the Mortal Realm." He rattles off thirty good animals. I keep trying to guess which ones the bad ones are. I'm constantly wrong. There is no pattern. Some animals go either way. Like, a horse is good, but it depends on the type of horse. Spiders that have less than eight legs are not only good but extremely important to our earth's survival. When I say that all spiders have eight legs, that's what makes them spiders, Doug is like, "That's not what makes them spiders," but he can't off the top of his head name one spider that doesn't have eight legs.

This goes on for two hours. One more hour, and Lucifer's champion starts destroying the world. I ask if this is written down anywhere, and he says yeah, and he hands me a three-ring binder, and I swear to God, I almost kick Doug into my fucking fence. I'm like, "What the fuck is wrong with you?" and he has no reasonable explanation. I'm about to go into my house when Doug calls out.

"Xandra begs to see you."

I'm like, look asshole, just point to where she is in the binder, and I'll see if she's at the zoo.

"Xandra's form is human. She works at Souplantation. You will know her. You two are bound together by…"

I stop listening to Doug. I'm thinking too hard about people I know at Souplantation. I got a lot of stuff on my mind, so the only person I remember at Souplantation is a dark-haired, big-tittied woman who makes the Manhattan Clam Chowder.

Doug is still talking, but I cut him off.

"Is she the dark-haired, big-tittied woman who makes the Manhattan Clam Chowder?"

"Yes," Doug says.

"Ok, cool."

"What about the other things I said about Xandra?" Doug asks.

"Fine. It's all fine."

27

"I only ask because, it's important that you understand the full connection between you and Xandra, and if you do not understand the connection, you risk losing to Lucifer's Champion."

"I got it."

"If you weren't paying attention—"

"—I was—"

"—Okay, but if you weren't, that's okay because I can explain it again. I cannot stress to you enough…"

I lose focus again. I would love to know how Souplantation transports all that soup. They can't make it in house. That's insane. They have to have an offsite location. But getting all that soup on a truck and not spilling it? You probably have to cool the soup down first. God, what a production. And then you get it to the restaurant, and you unload the truck…what then? Are you heating that soup back up? How? All at once?

I look down at my feet, and Doug is standing there. He hands me a seafoam green colored pill.

"Is this a gas station dick pill?" I ask. Doug looks legitimately hurt. He's taking in looks from the other animals, who are also shaking their heads.

"Greg, I'll explain it again—"

"—No. I'm joking, I get it. Xandra and me and the connection. Got it."

Doug keeps looking at me.

"I got it. No need to explain anymore," I say. I hold up the pill. "I'm going to keep this safe."

Doug is still looking at me.

"But I'm also going to use it."

Doug turns towards the fence, but looks back at me.

"But only when the time is right," I say.

Doug motions for the other animals to follow him under the fence. They follow.

Man, there are some no-shit gaps in what I understand about this situation. I'll take some blame. Not all of it. If he kept the IMAX thing going, we would be alright. But he didn't. Honestly, most, if not all, of the blame falls on him. Break up the learning. Have formal testing. Make me demonstrate my knowledge. Don't just ask me if I got it. What am I going to say, that I don't get it? I would never say that. Now, like always, I have to figure everything out on my own.

I know I have to go to Souplantation. They aren't open for much longer, so I've gotta move.

I go back inside the house and tell everyone I'm going to Souplantation. I tell everyone the rabbit and I spoke, and the rabbit said a lot of stuff. I say that I have to do something on behalf of Earth. There are some particulars pertaining to what I am supposed to do and the overall success of my mission, but I lost focus due to a bad learning curriculum. The rabbit said I have to talk to the big-tittied woman who works at Souplantation.

Ethan and my wife burst into tears. Ethan is crying because he wants to go to Souplantation, and he knows that I'm not going to take him because I never do. My wife is crying for the same reason she is always crying: I found a new way to disappoint her.

Danny says "whatever." I wish Danny would let himself feel hurt.

Before I leave, I keep the promise I made to myself a little while back. I sit for a little bit. Everybody is crying, but whatever. They get to stay home. Nice home. Air conditioning. Nintendo Switch. I give them a paradise to live in. Walk in my shoes. I'm getting jerked around by a rabbit, and I gotta kill some big-dicked beast from Hell.

Walk in my shoes.

Six

I get to Souplantation ten minutes before they close. Normally, that's not very good restaurant etiquette, but what I love about a Souplantation is all that nonsense goes right out the window. You can really slap a Souplantation around. Spit in its mouth. Nothing is better than taking a large group to a Souplantation and treating it like shit.

Souplantations are great. They are all the same. Salad. Bread. Muffins. Ice Cream. Four soups. Sodas. No alcohol, but if you want alcohol, you bring it yourself. Who stops you? No one. I bring two water bottles of vodka. One for pre-ice cream. One for post-ice cream.

There's a surprisingly large amount of people that want to show Souplantation a level of respect it has never deserved. Right when you walk in, you're supposed to grab a tray and make a little salad while they figure out where to let you sit. And people do it. Like fat little pigs waiting for mommy to wipe their asses.

Well this pig wipes his own ass. Fuck the salad line. I get a bowl and fill it with soup, and then I sit wherever the fuck I want to sit because Souplantation is my litter box, and I'm a cat who needs to shit!

I clearly suffered a head injury earlier today. But I've gotta keep moving.

I go through the side entrance of my local Souplantation and begin to do my usual. I am immediately harassed by some unsexy fifteen-year-old.

"You haven't paid sir! Please put the soup down."

"Fuck off."

They must have hired some local hardcore UFC fighters, because this kid gets his hands under my armpits fast. He jams my ass against the wall and slaps the vodka water bottles out of my left hand. Out of fear for my life, I drop the soup bowl and it lands on both of our groins. Me and the kid have hot soup on our balls. I scream, he doesn't. He then drags my ass to the back of the salad line and tells me to make a salad. I make a salad. My salad is cheese and ranch. Lettuce is always making people sick, and I've lost track of when it is safe to eat.

When I get to the end of the salad line where you have to pay, I tell the cashier that I'm a child and I want to pay a child's price. The fifteen-year-old tells the cashier that I'm a liar, that I am an old man, that he could smell my old-man breath when he was kicking my ass. I don't want to get my ass kicked again, so I say it's true, I'm a liar, and I should be charged fairly.

The fifteen-year-old seats me really far away from all the food. I ask for napkins, and he pushes his thumb into where my spine meets my head and I feel dizzy. He doesn't get me a napkin. I feel disgusting. I eat my cheese and ranch. Whatever.

I wait for the fifteen-year-old to clock out before I head for the soup area. Jesus. So many kids. I don't think Souplantation should be a place for kids. Kids don't need endless food. Adults do. Kids don't like soup. Adults do.

I check the soup menu. Chicken Noodle. Tortilla soup with chicken. Ok. Two chicken-based soups. Lazy. But I'm here for Manhattan Clam Chowder. You can't beat Manhattan Clam Chowder. It is criminal that Manhattan Clam Chowder has to take a backseat to New England Clam

Chowder. *Hey, you know what should be considered America's premier soup? Hot jizz with potatoes.* Get the fuck out of here.

I just remembered why I actually was supposed to go to Souplantation. I grab the closest Souplantation person. Really fast: another great thing about Souplantation. You are never having to run around trying to find an employee. They got them running around all over. You reach out your hand. You pull it back. Look at your hand: I guarantee you have a Souplantation employee in your fingers. Fishing with dynamite.

I reach for the first guy I see wearing a black polo shirt and get him by the back of the neck. I swing him around to get his attention. Sure enough, he's a Souplantation guy. Now, he must be related to that other kid because he takes my head and bounces it off the sneeze guard before I can get my question out. Souplantation has changed.

He bounces my head a couple times, and it looks like that's what he's gonna want to do for the rest of the night. I manage to yell "Xandra" between bounces, so I get my point across.

I hear a voice behind me. "Zquartog," the voice says. I've heard that name before, but when I hear it this time the center of my chest feels a beautiful, cold light. Why? Who cares.

The bouncing stops. I turn around.

Yeah. There she is. Xandra. She's in a pretty standard Souplantation outfit. Her name tag says "Alexis." She looks like she knows everything about Manhattan Clam Chowder and a whole lot of other things too. Souplantation feels smaller. It's dumb, but I feel as if I have spent multiple lives with her? I dunno.

And, I'm not trying to be crass, but I am really vibing off of her big titties. They seem like the safest place in the world. I don't want to climb up a bleeding tower. I don't want to fight that circumcised demon. I want to lay on Xandra's stomach perpendicularly, then rest her big titties over my body like two little blankets. I want to hit a REM cycle that makes people think I am a vegetable.

"Xandra," I say. She smiles. Jesus, it's a great smile. It's the kind of smile that makes me so mad at Debra. I can't believe I'm married to my stupid wife. She's at home crying about a bunch of nonsense, and I got Xandra smiling at me like we are beginning a new chapter of something with precious and ancient roots. Why me.

"I am about to take my ten. Come outside with me?" Xandra itches her breast. I'm conflicted. I want to be near her, in a way that can only be described as always and forever. But I'm this close to the soup, and I'd love some soup. If I had a bowl of Manhattan Clam in me, I think it would really put me in the right mindset. So what happens when I come back from that break, and there is no more Manhattan Clam? This Souplantation trip would be useless. I mean, not useless, but close. Basically useless.

Xandra smiles. "I have Manhattan Clam Chowder at my studio apartment. I make it from scratch. All the ingredients are from Whole Foods." Clearly, she did a thought reading. I've already said how I feel about thought reading and how it makes you no better than Mel Gibson, but I'm trying not to get wrapped up in that.

And it's easy, because I am in the early stages of having a big-time erection based on my feelings for Xandra. I feel the back side of my penis shaft fill with blood. The Manhattan Clam Chowder with Whole Foods ingredients is putting the blood in my penis meat at double my normal speed. Whole Foods doesn't fuck around. I don't go there because it's intimidating, but I use their parking lot for when I go to FedEx.

Xandra doesn't wait for me to respond. She walks through the swinging doors into the kitchen. I follow her.

The first thing I notice is this kitchen doesn't have a doggie bed. I'm disappointed. I'm pretty tired, and it would be nice to power down for a second.

Next thing, nobody is really cooking. There are four—God, how do you say this—voids? Just four black voids where I thought there would be cooking stuff, and occasionally, someone will reach into one of the voids and close their eyes, and when they open their eyes and pull back their hand, it is filled with a tin cannister of soup. I would be impressed, but I remember that I saw two chicken-based soups out front. If you are going to have voids, have the voids communicate. I don't know.

I make it outside. Xandra is sitting on the stairs. She motions for me to sit next to her. I do. We stare into each other's eyes, and whatever, it's magical. It's like learning you have a part of your heart missing and that you found the missing piece all at the same time. Big deal.

"Here we are again," she says. She seems tired.

I say, *"Huh?"* She smiles. It's a smile that implies that I am kind of stupid, but whatever.

"You saw the Bleeding Tower?" she asks.

"Yeah."

"Are you going to enter it?"

"Well, yeah."

"And you will fight Lucifer's Champion?"

"Yeah, I gotta be there in, like, eight minutes."

Xandra doesn't look tired anymore. She looks sad. Old. Man, I know it's the wrong time to say it, but it would be outstanding to hold one of her titties. Just to see. What's the feel? Soft? Heavy? Light? You would think that—

"You can hold one," she says. I do.

Man, perfect titty. She knows it, too. But she's got an outstanding attitude about it, so everything is really great. She still seems sad, though. Typically, when women are unhappy, I ask them to give me a smile, but I want to treat her differently.

"You're gonna be fine," I say, romantically. A single tear falls down her face. She's got something in her head that is gonna come out of her mouth, and even though context clues are telling me it's going to be bad, my street smarts tell me I should be pretty excited.

"You don't have to fight this time," she says. I am confused. So I say that I am confused. I tell her it is her responsibility to make me not confused anymore. I really lay into her.

"You have climbed that tower before," she says.

I haven't. So she is a liar now. Great. Another woman who lies. "That is the first time I've seen that tower. Ever," I say.

"In this life." She is looking off into the distance. I have reached my brain amount, so I close my eyes and try to fall asleep. I feel her move towards me. She's in my personal bubble. I smell her clam-infused breath.

"Did Doug tell you about the connection between you and I?" Xandra asks me.

"No," I say.

Xandra bites some loose skin around her thumb. "That doesn't sound like Doug," she says.

"Yeah, but Doug has a way about him, you know?"

"We would have nothing without the work Doug has put in."

"Yeah, but what do we have that is so great?"

"Hope."

I try to fart, but my leg goes into spasm. I stand up and shake my leg out a bit. I sit back down.

"I can't believe Doug didn't tell me about the connection between us. If you know why it is special, you can tell me, but I definitely want an explanation from Doug on why he dropped the ball."

Xandra stops biting her thumb skin. She swallows whatever skin she had in her mouth.

"Every person on Earth falls on a spectrum of good and evil—"

"—I heard this part. Skip this part."

"Okay. At the center—"

"—is us. We're the center of good and evil. Balance. Skip this part."

"Okay. So you know about the balance part. On Earth. What about other universes?"

"Like what? The moon?"

"No, the moon is part of this universe."

"Mars."

"That's a part of this universe, too."

"Okay, well, Doug said Mars was a different universe, so I'm only repeating what Doug told me."

"Greg," Xandra's soft hand touches mine. I touched this hand in my shower accident dream.

"We are the balance for all universes."

She looks down at her slip-on Vans. "We were, at least." When she looks back up at me, her eyes are wet. "Every time I see you and you don't remember what happened, a part of me dies. When you died—"

"What—"

"Zquartog—please remember!" This time she doesn't grab my hand, but does an open-handed push against my sternum. Everything goes black.

I'm being born from nothing. Something is being born next to me. It's Xandra. We both see each other. Even though we are little spirit babies, we don't look like spirit babies. We're both really turning each other on. It's very mystical and spiritual, but there is a heavy undertone of, "this is not incest so, really go nuts on each other."

And we do. To call it fucking would be the wrong word. I don't think there is a word for it, so I'll call it qfucking. We're qfucking in darkness.

We're given a bag. Looks like a bag of marbles. I would have to guess, like, 39 marbles in the bag. Okay. Fine.

Xandra and I open these bags and we stretch these marbles out into big ass marbles. Huge. Size of Earth, I'm guessing. One actually looks like Earth. I'm looking at them like, "Man these are great!" but Xandra is like, "Hey, we gotta connect these stupid things." Why? I don't know. But we do.

More qfucking. More qfucking. Then there's a big flash and I open my eyes and close my eyes, and every time I open my eyes, I am being born again but in different places. This happens, I'm guessing, 38 times. I also have this thing where I run into Xandra and she calls me Zquartog and she is crying and she tells me not to go somewhere, but I do, and that happens maybe 37 times? Again, rough numbers, but I feel like I'm close.

I feel Xandra's hand leave my chest, and I'm back to sitting next to her.

"I'm sorry," she says. "But I had to show you."

I don't know what the fuck she just showed me, but I nod my head.

"You have climbed that tower 38 times. You have fallen to Lucifer's Champion 38 times. Lucifer has taken the Mortal Realm of 38 universes. This is the last universe. Please, Zquartog! Please—"

She stops speaking. Thank God. I bet what she just said is not true. I say something like, "There's no way I have lost 38 fights to one guy. I call bullshit," and she bursts into tears. Tears mean truth, so, shit: I've done this 38 times. And lost.

Xandra grabs my shirt with both hands.

"You can't win, Zquartog. But you don't have to fight."

"Doug says I have to fight. And he says I can win."

"Is it a guarantee? Can Doug guarantee that you can come home to me?"

Xandra has got a real desperate look on her face. In my experience, the only time I see that face are on the people who are choosing to be sexually intimate with me. So, all this shit with Doug and the Lucifer's Champion are gonna have to pause for a second.

I do my best listening, starting now.

"If you don't fight, we can stay together. When war starts, we can run. We can hide. Wars take years. Decades. We can have decades, Zquartog! We can, for once in our many lives, be cowards and enjoy ourselves. We can enjoy the spoils of each other."

She puts my second hand on her second titty. I'm fully erect. I've got gym shorts on, but my dick is so thin that there is not enough base support to allow my erection to pop up my gym shorts comedically. It bends pretty bad, but, if anyone is used to this, it's me.

"If you climb the tower this time and fall at his sword, I don't know what happens after that. No one does."

This is the first time I heard this guy has a sword. Great. At home, I've got a pretty big Cutco knife, and Ethan's got a Nerf gun that shoots faster than a Nerf gun should probably shoot. Sounds like I need both.

Or I don't. I'm fading in and out of what Xandra is saying, but I think she wants us to hump like pigs until Hell defeats Earth. It seems entirely irresponsible, but I have both my hands on the Michael Jordan of human titties. If being responsible means I've got to ungrip these bad boys, I am a permanently irresponsible fuck.

I tell her that if this is all real and we are some type of soulmates who have lived in multiple universes together, then I think me seeing one of her nipples is not a huge deal. She comes back with, well I'm still at work. And I'm like, you want to spend the final days of the last remaining universe working a night shift at Souplantation? She laughs and is like, good point Zquartog, and we go walk to the parking lot to find our cars. We're flirty, and I am putting on a perfectly healthy Joe Biden-type charm, so everything is 94%above board. I tell her that we can't go to my place because I have a full-blown family that includes a wife. Xandra says her place is fine. I ask what kind of mattress she has, and she says I don't know, and I know that means we got a problem.

Hey, people trying to pass off as adults: if you don't know whether you have a Tempur-Pedic or not, you do not have a Tempur-Pedic. Great. So it looks like I'm going home to get my Tempur-Pedicmattress. Xandra doesn't seem too happy about this, but if I am going to even think about waiting out the war between Hell and Earth, I'm not doing it on some bullshit IKEA twin.

Also, again, I hate to be crass, but the leverage I get from a Tempur-Pedic mattress is outstanding. By leverage, I mean for sex stuff. You can really dig your feet and knees in. My dick is real thin, so it slides out a lot. If I don't have traction to keep me grounded, you might as well put me in one of those penis cages and let some other guy do the dirty work.

I tell Xandra to give me her address. I also tell her to calm down. She hasn't explicitly done anything to warrant this, but sometimes I feel like I need to say that to women. I get in my car and head home.

Seven

I pull my car in my driveway. I know this conversation is going to be tough, so I gotta choose my words carefully. I think about it for a little bit and decide that the best thing to do is not let anyone speak except for me.

I go around the back and come through the screen door. What's my favorite book? *Art of War*. Sun Tzu. I haven't finished it, but I know that you should always be throwing people off. Also, if you do a war, you should win it. Seems obvious, but it was written a long time ago, so people were dumber than they are now.

I make a ton of noise coming through the screen door. Bam! Dominate the space. That's not Sun Tzu. That might be me.

My wife is looking at our wedding album. Danny is peeling the wrapper off something. Ethan is deep-throating a popsicle. I hit everyone with a preemptive "Knock it off." Debra starts crying, again. Ethan chokes on his popsicle a little, and the sound haunts me. Danny keeps peeling the wrapper. He doesn't know I exist. Come on, Danny. Let your father in.

I make it very clear and brief: "I have a soulmate. Her name is Xandra. We have an intense relationship that goes beyond the boundaries of this universe. I am going to leave this home to go hang out with her in her studio apartment. I need to grab the Tempur-

Pedicmattress because we most likely will be having sex. I require leverage and grip for my skinny penis."

I look at my sons. "Your father has a skinny penis."

My wife does a banshee scream. "YOU'RE JUST LIKE EVERY OTHER MAN."

Oh, shut up, Debra. Do you hear the demons chanting my name? I'm clearly not. I leave the room because I am bored.

I go upstairs to our bedroom. God, what a nice bed. King size. Tempur-Pedic. Instant cool technology. I go to lift it. Doesn't budge. I am immediately feeling self-conscious about my masculinity. I can't lift a mattress, and I'm supposed to put Xandra on top of the mattress and make love to her? Jesus.

I call down to Danny to help with the mattress. He says, "I don't know."

That's not how you answer that question, Danny. Listen to your father. Hear my voice.

He comes up, surprisingly. We try to lift the mattress. We can't. I say to him, "Doesn't it suck that we are both failing at being true men?" He moves his hair out of his eyes and shrugs. Great.

I call down to my wife to help me move the bed. She is crying so hard that she is coughing. I tell her to cover her mouth. I don't need to get sick. We can get it off the box spring, but we can only move it four feet before it goes to the ground. I raise my voice at my wife in the way that a coach would yell at one of their players they can't stand—motivating but dismissive. Nothing.

I don't even bother calling down to Ethan. If I call down to Ethan, he will pretend I didn't say anything, or he will respond back by trying to tell me about his day.

So I go down to get Ethan. He—Jesus fuck—is outside unrolling a slip and slide. He sees me and thinks that I'm not going to flip out because he got my bathing suit out of the laundry room. I think, in this environment, with this kind of pressure, I could hit Ethan and get away with it. I don't. Relax.

He set the slip and slide up fast enough, so I let him do a couple of slops. He's pretty good at it. I tell him to run a little faster. He skids out into the grass and cries because the grass-stained his tummy. I tell him to put on a shirt and go up to my bedroom to help me move the mattress.

We fold the Tempur-Pedic mattress in my car. I keep wanting to talk about Xandra, but no one wants to talk about it. I get it, but I also don't get it, you know? Be happy for your friends. I give everyone a side hug and drive to Xandra's.

Eight

Xandra's place is right on a golf course. Par 3, so she's still poor. But a nice view: her place is right next to the green. I figure, after I make love to my soulmate, I could do some chip and putt practice.

I do a quick look at the sand trap. If it's too deep, I won't bother going home to get my sand wedge.

Interesting. Dead body right at the bottom of the trap. Actually, it's probably worth mentioning. I saw a fair number of dead bodies on the drive over. Like, four. Not a huge number, but when you think of dead bodies you see on a typical drive, pretty high. And I can tell—I can always tell—these were suicide. And I'm like, *the sky goes red, you see some monsters flying in the air, and it's a little too much?* Loser.

I walk through a patch of flowers to get to Xandra's front door. No welcome mat. Her mailbox is filled with envelopes. Jesus. Empty your mailbox.

I go through her mail. A lot of bill collectors. Insane amount of people trying to sue her. Credit card fraud. One is a class action lawsuit that claims she took money for a scholarship designed to support kids whose parents died in a tsunami. Thirty kids with dead tsunami parents signed the thing.

My first impulse is to really judge her, but my street smarts say "I dunno." If you think about everything—how many people usually die in tsunamis, how many people apply for scholarships, how many people are actually smart enough to go to college—I'm on Xandra's side. If Xandra would let me, I would almost want to write back to these kids and say, "Hey, tsunami kids, do you really think you should be thinking about college? Take some time. Work on yourself. Maybe put your heads together and think about how you're gonna stop the next tsunami." And, you know, just thinking about what Doug said: if Xandra and I are the moral center of the universe, that means there are people a lot worse than Xandra. I bet there's a guy who actually started the tsunami. Sue him!

I knock on the door. Door opens. There is Xandra. She is in a robe. I see a real tasteful inside titty draped over her stomach. I tell her that I'd like to shower because earlier today I shit all over myself. She giggles. She invites me to come inside. So I do.

There's something about a studio apartment that makes me want to blow my brains out. But Xandra's is not bad. I mean, I think everyone should try and get in a five-bed, four-bath situation, but whatever.

Every single picture on her walls is the Bob Seger album cover that had "Night Moves" on it. Xandra gets it. You get a group of geniuses together and give them instruments, and they are coming out with "Night Moves". Do I need every poster in my house to be "Night Moves"? Probably not. But I feel safe.

I get to the bathroom. Nice shower. Shower knobs turn easy, but have a little authority to them. Water turns on. Good flow. Couple streams are out of place, but it's not enough to stop showering.

The real pearl is the complete surface shower mat. I can't stand anywhere in this shower without standing on shower mat. The shower mat has grips that are invested in your safety. And thank God, because I am four controlled breaths into a downward dog. This time, I do roll into a bridge for a particular reason. I mentioned earlier that a bridge stretches out my lower back, but it also unlocks my hips. I need hips for sex. Tight hips, and I cum way too early. The looser the hips, the longer I last.

I get ten more controlled breaths. Hips feel great. I turn off the shower. I go to reach for a towel. No towel.

But Xandra is standing there. Her robe is kind of open. I can see a nipple, but honestly, I'm so caught up in everything that I am like, we are beyond nipples. We are two souls, you stupid bitch.

With her hands, she wrings the water off my flaccid penis. This involves twisting my penis. I do scream. But in the end, I have a good, dry penis. The rest of my body is soaking wet. Xandra smiles and leaves the bathroom so I guess I'm supposed to stay wet.

Man, what the fuck. This is going to be big-time sex stuff. I go through my pants to find my phone. Phone needs to be on silent. Most phone alerts take me out of sex instantly. Some lock me into sex harder, but I'm not rolling the dice.

Before I find my phone, I get my hands on something else. It's like a seafoam green color. Looks like a gas station sex pill. If this thing wasn't a gas station sex pill, no one said anything to me. And if this thing is a gas station sex pill, now would be the time to take it.

I dry swallow the gas station sex pill. Outstanding. I leave the shower.

Xandra's bedroom has one of those poor-people dividers that poor people use to make a room when they don't actually have a room. I always say, you want a room? Buy a room. But I'm not going to say that to Xandra.

Her "bedroom" looks soft. Like, well, titties. And before anyone jumps down my throat, her walls and bed are skin colored, and her pillows are shaped like two nipples. She likes her titties just as much as I do.

She sits me on the bed. She goes to a desk in the corner and fucks around on her iPhone.

45

"I just found this torrent that has all the 'Night Moves' covers." She plays the first one. John Mellencamp. I can tell the sex between us is going to be mega passionate. Almost violent. That's what Mellencamp does. I feel a dribble of precum escape my penis. For the first time in my life, I pray. I realize that there is no God because if there were a God, they would have come down and knocked that tower back underground. And if they didn't, they wouldn't be worth praying to. So I pray to me. Moral Center Guy.

Xandra sits next to me. We lock eyes. This is big-time sexual compatibility. Every time I go home, people are screaming and crying, but when I look at Xandra, I hear nothing. She is peace and quiet.

Before I know it, we are mouth kissing. One of us clearly had some more Manhattan Clam Chowder. We're licking each other's tongues with our mouths pushed together, so I'm getting a hot breath with some unchewed chowder nuggets. My dick is so jam-packed with blood that I feel a reserve pool resting in my pubic region. I got like a little water balloon of blood just above my dick shaft. Very sensitive to the touch. The kissing is great. The gas station dick pill is better.

Her hands are everywhere. What a beast. I can't keep up. At one point she grabs my wrist so hard that I lose feeling in my hand and it goes limp. Then she uses my limp hand to go under my gym shorts and cup my scrotum. Super smart because now she's got two of her own hands to work some other parts of my body.

Me? I got my free hand on her right nipple. I don't remember if I read this in a book or dreamt it, but women like when you pull their nipple tips towards you. So that's what I'm doing. And, I don't know if she is peeing or her juice valves are going bananas, but she seems pretty comfortable.

She's got a deep, fluid breath going. It's sexy and also a health concern. She's a big girl, and she's going full force. Slap-the-floor, all-four-quarters type shit. It's not my place to tell someone that they are overdoing it. But it sounds like the breath of someone who might die. I'm doing fine. I got a little back-of-the-neck sweat, but I'm pacing myself.

We stop mouth kissing. Our faces are covered in spit and food. We're thick and wet and ready to do damage. She wrings my dick out again. Didn't think it warranted that, but, a little water came out. Again, extremely painful.

Xandra bends down over my dick and balls and puts all of them in her mouth at once. She's lashing her tongue around and making very low humming noises. The vibrations and jabbing of her tongue is making my thighs cramp. I feel a wet dew starting to come over my blood balloon.

Please. Don't cum.

She lifts up, almost as if she knows that was too much and it was, in fact, her fault. She lets me pace around the room to walk my jizz-tremors out.

She slides further into her bed. She pulls her legs apart. There is a sound when that happens. Like two wet pieces of ham being pulled off each other. She spreads her vagina lips very quickly with one hand. The other hand is pointing towards the correct hole. I appreciate that.

I am done pacing. I wade into the bed. My dick knows precisely where to go. The neck sweat feels cool because a fan is blowing on me now. Butt-naked on the cusp of humping, and you sneak off to turn on a fan? What a legend.

I'm hovering over her body. My 35 pushups a day is really paying off. Very minimal shaking.

She grabs my dick. This time, she does not wring it of liquid. She smooshes it into her vagina. I'm like a greyhound once they see the toy rabbit: I go as fast as humanly possible. That's Sex 101, baby.

Our bodies are two strobe lights. I feel our two creamy white figures slapping up against each other in the night. I hear pockets of air between us burst and make little fart noises. Our sweat collides and solidifies into small salt rocks, cutting us open and making our bodies sting. Occasionally, I scream things like, "Rock N' Roll!" or "Winner Winner, Chicken Dinner!" We are really clicking.

I lose track of time. Time can go fuck itself. The only sense of rhythm I haveis the mashing of my pubic bone against her hips. We stay in missionary because we both know that other positions are a big waste of time. If I ever get bored, I can drown my face in her perfect titties, and I have life again.

I feel my calves start to cramp up. A thin yellow film of sweat begins to drip from my neck. I am prepared to cum big time.

I pull out of Xandra's vagina like a rocket. I explode. Thick, chunky ropes. Xandra is clapping, really whooping it up for me. You know you found your soulmate when you don't even have to explain that you prefer to pull out. I feel the blood vessels burst in my eyes. All the organs in my body squeeze for dear life. Once the last rope leaves my dick head, my organs rest. I rest.

I look down at my dick. It is a broken mess. I ask Xandra if she came. She says she was close. I smile. Close is pretty good.

I ask her what time it is. She says, "It's morning, fifteen years in the future."

Oh, come on.

Fuck.

Nine

I don't want to be mad at her because we just did some good fucking, but at some point in the past fifteen years, you didn't want to say, *hey, I know you were planning on being somewhere, just want to give you a quick mid-hump-sesh time update?*

I find a couple towels to wipe up fifteen years of cum with. My genitals look insane. She's laying on the bed trying to get me to stay.

"Please, my love, he'll kill you."

I look at her and say, "Relax. I don't even know if he is still there. It's been fifteen years, and I told him I'd be back in two, maybe three hours. He might have gone home. I would have."

"No. He is waiting for you, Zquartog. He has to kill one of us. He knows he can kill you. He will stay at the tower until you return," she says.

"Well, I mean, does he know if he can kill you?"

Xandra shakes her head no.

I ask, "Why does he not know if he can kill you?"

"I've never attempted to challenge him."

Okay. Here we go. You want equality and feminism, but we have gone through 38 universes, and you have never offered to fight this asshole? Okay. No. Good for you.

Then she says her and I are technically genderless and I say, "Well, explain this," and I grab my dick, but it is in a terrible amount of pain. I yell "Tie!" because I believe the argument was a tie.

I find my gym shorts and I cobble together a makeshift protein shake from shit I see in Xandra's kitchen area. God, what a shitty apartment. I'm not sure what is going to happen once I get in that tower, but it would be good to get a little pump. Maybe even some cardio. I look at myself in the mirror. I must have lost 85 pounds. The sex ruined my body. I am covered in bruises. My face looks like a skeleton. I take a drink of the protein shake I made. Terrible. All the ingredients are fifteen years old. Hard boiled eggs. Awful.

Xandra is watching me trying to get my shit together. I'm not trying to get back into this whole prophecy thing. Not yet. One thing at a time. I do not have a shirt that will fit me. I think for twenty seconds. Nothing. I have no productive thoughts. I will go shirtless.

Feet are still feet, so my shoes still fit. I notice my gym shorts are falling down to my ankles anytime I move too much. I'm not fighting anyone with my dick out. Fuck. I'll have to borrow clothes from Ethan.

Jesus. Ethan is what, 24 now? Danny is 31? My wife is probably around the same age. Do we still have a home?

I turn to Xandra, hoping I can capture the moment and find closure for this chapter of our romance: "Bye-bye time." She looks at me in a way that does not seem promising.

"Is that all you have to say to me?" she says. I can see her lips tremble. I pause.

"I can do a couple of mouth kisses. Not a lot, though. I just worked through a lot of shit in my head, and I got to get moving." So we mouth kiss. Super great. I go to touch a titty, and she stops me. I look at her like, *I just had fifteen years of titty touching, and now we're done?* And she's looking back at me like I'm some kind of an asshole. But then her face becomes nicer. She smiles, but still no titty

"Leave a key under the mat for me. I'm going to beat his ass." I say that to Xandra. We both acknowledge that, despite our knowledge of how this will probably turn out, what I said was awesome. One more mouth kiss. I leave her house.

Ten

My car is still outside. A couple of parking tickets, which seems insensitive. I check out the sand trap. A lot more dead bodies in the sand trap. I feel no desire to work on my chipping and putting.

It's for sure daytime, but the sky is not blue. Still very, very red. Winged creatures are also still flying around. They are a little closer, but not much. Still chanting my name. What a joke.

The drive back to my house is pretty grim. A lot of signs are spray painted over. Every Jamba Juice I see is closed. There's a bunch of empty cars all over the middle of the street. Some of them have dead bodies in them, and some don't, but it's not like I'm counting or anything. It's a lot. But I also see other people going about their day pretty normal, so, I dunno. Could be worse.

My house looks the same. In fact, probably a little better. I never did any major repairs because after the French drain incident, I couldn't emotionally handle reading directions or any minor setbacks. The door is unlocked, so I go inside. I go front door this time because, well, I've been gone fifteen years. Me being back is surprising enough.

I expect screams and crying. I hear nothing. I move quick to the kitchen, in case they were planning on surprising me. I will never be surprised.

Bam! I move in quick with big, physical gestures only to see a super polite Asian family having a sit-down breakfast. I freak them out. The dad comes at me, but one of my big physical gestures coming in was a chest-level punch. That punch lands, and lands good. I gain a ton of confidence due to this immediate success, and pretty soon I am fighting every person in this house. I am doing a fantastic job. Lot of people in this family are getting punched hard, and eventually they stop getting up. I get to speak, finally.

"You are not my family. Where is my family?"

"Who are you," the Dad asks.

"I'm Greg Maxwell, GM of the San Diego Padres and Moral Center of the Earth."

"Mr. Maxwell—do you know Danny?"

When you lose 85 pounds, you really feel the lump in your throat. *I do know Danny, dad of Asian family, I really do.*

Okay, so get this: Danny took this fifteen years like a champ. Danny became a bit of a slum lord and started buying up foreclosed properties in the area. Now he's like an apocalypse landlord-type person. People say Danny is "tough but fair," out of fear that he is going to make them homeless. I hear the dad tell me this and I have to excuse myself, so I can go to the bathroom and cry tears of joy for my beautiful son. I know where the bathroom is because I used to live in this house with my family.

My son, owning and leasing properties. Jesus. What a stud.

The Asian family gives me Danny's contact information. I finish up breakfast with them. We make bonds that go beyond race and culture. I take a shit in their bathroom and leave.

Eleven

D anny lives a little west of Rancho Bernardo in a place called 4S Ranch. That's the real name of a city. Apparently, they had a big dirt lot called 4S, and they built some houses on it, and when it came time to be a neighborhood, someone with enough common sense said "Hey, we printed out all these documents that say 4S on them. We're done. That's the name." Then they threw "Ranch" on the end and, hey, that's a city. We give out medals for so much stupid shit, but this person honestly deserves one. Just good, practical thought.

I pull up to Danny's home. It is nice. The lump in my throat is still kicking. I knock on the door, and a beautiful woman answers the door. Her eyes go wide, and she screams for Danny. That could be for several reasons. I am a naked stranger. I am 100 pounds.

Danny comes down a flight of stairs and sees me.

"Dad?"

"Yeah," I say. "Dad is back to raise you. I'm here to make sure you grow up good."

"I'm 31 years old. You're a naked, starving person. Go fuck yourself."

Danny says this, which hurts, but he invites me inside.

He sits me down in a second living room that he calls a parlor. I did not teach him that word. Interesting. He seems like he's in a bad mood. I ask him if the ol' wife is giving him any grief today.

"Dad, you not only abandoned our family, you abandoned Earth. I feel an anger toward you that is insane. You are a shitty, useless person." He's trembling. I'm still not sure why he's mad. I shrug.

"Hey, some days are better than others, I guess," is what I say back. His wife—my daughter in law?—screams something like "Listen to your son," or something. I dunno, I'm not paying a whole lot of attention. The ceilings in this house are crazy high. Good, high ceilings. And the walls seem thick. Some homes in San Diego think they can get away with no insulation, but let me tell you, my friend, you have got to insulate your house. No excuses.

I ask Danny where everyone is. This makes him madder. This kid's a ticking time bomb. Like, for starters, where is my wife?

Danny tells me that Debra lost her marbles right after I forced her and her two children to load her marital bed into my car so I could have sex with a woman I just met at a Souplantation. This psychological breakdown led her to convince herself that she and I just got engaged to be married. She planned our wedding for a year and a half. She drained our joint bank account to throw lavish engagement parties and pay for wedding vendors.

"Apparently," Danny says, "she is still in the Marriott Marquis at the rooftop venue waiting for you to come down the aisle. She's been there for 12 years."

I don't like to use this language, but what a stupid bitch. I ask where Ethan is.

"Gone," Danny says. "He took his Nerf gun and left." Good, I think. Not great because I was going to use the Nerf gun. But he's nine, so it's not like he can go buy Nerf guns.

Jesus, wait. He is 24. He can buy his own Nerf guns. I tell Danny that if Ethan shows up, get my Nerf gun back.

Danny asks me when I am going to fight Lucifer's Champion.

"How do you know about that?"

"Everyone on Earth knows you are supposed to fight him. He broadcasts it every day. The—things—they have been chanting your name for fifteen years," Danny says.

Honestly, everyone needs to stop caring about this shit so much. Take a break. I tell Danny I'm not fighting anyone butt-naked. Danny is built like a goddamn bull now, so I can't wear his clothes. They have no kids. I'm not a grandpa? Whatever.

We land on his wife's clothes. Her name is Jen, by the way. She wears pretty gender-neutral stuff. I get some corduroys and a beautiful silk button-up. She hates that I am wearing her clothes, and I'm like, "I don't think I'm going to be doing much jujitsu on this guy, so I think the clothes won't get dirty on the ground." Then she says stuff like, "No, it's you. You ruined your son, and you are a bad person," and Danny has to pull her away and it's all kind of shrill, you know? I ask Danny if he has any Cutco knives, and he says no. I tell him that whatever knives he has are inferior to Cutco knives and that he should have Cutco knives.

Danny walks me out the front door. No hug, which is tough. But I have clothes now. I'm good to go. The door behind me closes really fast. They got some good grease on those hinges.

Twelve

I drive over to the 24Hr Fitness parking lot. At this point, I am driving on a mix of road and human bodies. Every once in a while, an animated corpse of a coyote runs in front of my bumper. By the time I get to 24Hr Fitness, my car is a wreck.

God, I'd love to get a workout in. But 24Hr Fitness looks really, really closed.

And, yeah, the tower is still there. Bleeding like a motherfucker. And I see that stupid black cloud. I know that hooved asshole is on it. I say some stuff in my head to test him.

If you fly on a cloud, you are a massive dipshit.

"GREG MAXWELL. ARE YOU HERE TO STOP MY DESTRUCTION AND CHALLENGE ME IN COMBAT?"

Hold on, I'm seeing a lot of people who have killed themselves. I respect you a little bit, so I am hoping you are not considering suicides as part of your body count. What have you actually destroyed?

"I have led my army straight to the heart of the most powerful country on Earth. I have destroyed NEBRASKA."

I bust up. What a joke.

Holy shit, guy. You had 15 years, and you went after Nebraska? Garbage decision making.

"I have seized the heart of the world's kingdom. This United States will cease to be united without its center!"

Oh my God. What a fucking loser. *So, what's next?*

"IOWA."

What a bum! I walk back to my car. I see his little cloud move towards me. It's a cloud, so it moves at cloud speed. "GREG MAXWELL, YOU WALK AWAY FROM COMBAT? IS EARTH'S CHAMPION A COWARD?"

I'm like, *no asshole, but it looks like I got a little more time to kill. You can have Iowa. After Iowa, consider Indiana, or Kansas. I don't give a shit. Fuck, if you weren't such a dick, I'd help you with Kansas. But here's the deal, big guy: I am 100 pounds right now. I have upset my soulmate. I'm learning things about myself, and I'd like to slow the pace down a bit. I'm gonna go on vacation, clear my head, hang out with some of my boys, recharge. Then when I'm ready to come back, I'm gonna come back, tan, beefed out, and I'm gonna tear your fucking head off.*

Lucifer's Champion almost falls off his cloud he's so pissed. He's like, "NO. WE FIGHT NOW. ASCEND MY TOWER." I put my hands up like, "Enough." *My car has got a V8 Engine. You're on a cloud. Sit tight, asshole.*

I drive away. I have some errands to run.

Thirteen

I mentioned earlier that I have a gig as the General Manager of the San Diego Padres. It's a paycheck. It keeps the lights on and food on my plate. Well, one time my wife said something about me, and it hurt my feelings, so I decided to open up a mutual account and auto deposit 10%of my paycheck. Whatever. I make like, I dunno, 2.4 million a year. People say 2.4 is not blue-collar stuff, but I think its blue-collar stuff.

Turns out, I kept my job while I was with Xandra. Apparently, we did pretty well. We being the San Diego Padres. Won a couple championships. By a couple, I mean thirteen. I like to think I set the team up for success. Most people inside and outside the organization would most likely say otherwise, but I dunno.

Anyway, I had this thing in my contract that says if we ever win the championship, my pay doubles. Contracts are weird. We won a lot of championships, so my pay doubled a lot. Still blue-collar stuff, but it's nice. Now, this is just back of napkin math, but I made about 19.6 billion dollars in 13 years. I guess I didn't get paid in years 14 and 15 because my contract destroyed Major League Baseball and professional baseball no longer exists? Hey, I don't do this job as a charity. I gotta get paid.

I say all this because right now I am at the credit union that holds this mutual account. Ten percent of 19.6 billion. Growing at a conservative return of 5% compounded yearly? I dunno. Should have, again, rough math, about 2.4 billion?

So yeah, the owner of the Credit Union I am at is crying because I am holding a withdrawal request of 2.4 billion dollars. Big time crying. He's fucking hysterical. Apparently, if I were to pull out my money, I would put every single one of his branches out of business, causing the entire San Diego community to go into an insurmountable depression. I'm telling him, whatever, you can give me the bars of gold in the back if it makes it easier. But I'm going to walk out of here with my 2.4 billion. It's the end of days, and I am going to continue to trust credit unions? Fuck off.

Also, me and The Boys need scratch to party.

I haven't talked about The Boys in detail yet. I try not to because it's truly a bond that most people are too stupid to understand. Because everyone is so stupid, it makes me really guarded and emotional. Like, imagine loving something so much it hurt you. But not your kids or your wife, because that's not real hurt. Okay, now imagine something more powerful than what you imagined. You can't. That's what I'm talking about when I say people are too stupid. But if you have to know anything, know this: if I am going to party, I need The Boys.

The following people I would define as "The Boys":

Eddie "Scary Mask" Dumpino – Childhood friend. Real rat-faced, wimpy, not super cool or funny, you know? Great guy. He makes these handmade Halloween masks for a living. Hasn't sold any. Crazy poor. He's always calling us up saying he is moments from death and that he hasn't eaten anything in weeks. But let me tell you something: the guy can rally.

Frank Thomas – Yeah, the guy from the testosterone commercials. And before you ask, of course he banged all the girls in the commercial. But before the testosterone commercials, he was a pretty decent ballplayer and just an overall beast to party with. I met him when I accidentally walked into the visitors' locker room when his team was playing the Padres. Got to watch him towel off. What a man. We bonded over that moment and other moments when I accidentally walked into the visitors' locker room.

Sammo Hung – Pretty prominent Chinese actor. Was like a fat Jackie Chan. I guess he still is a fat Jackie Chan because he is still fat. But the reason he is fat is the reason why he is fun to party with: the guy likes to fucking party. Imagine doing sake bombs with someone who at any point could kick your dick up into your skull. Wild shit. The only downside to Sammo is that he is not Jackie Chan. And, as much as you try, you can't get him to pretend he is Jackie Chan. Takes offense to that. Super sensitive.

Kevin Madsen – Pretty normal guy. Wife. Big, beautiful family. Lives in Nebraska. Couldn't get a hold of him.

Everyone except Kevin is game. Don't even need to say the spot. If you have a couple billion dollars in your pocket, and you want to feel some fucking action, you are flying into Boston's Logan Airport, renting a car, and driving an hour and a half to Cape Cod. Specifically, Hyannis.

You can fly into Barnstable Airport, but why? Get the car. Make the drive. Let yourself have the moment where you cross the Bourne Bridge with your boys and officially enter the poon grotto that is The Cape.

We all land in Logan. Split a rental car. This breaks Scary Mask. Dumped his life savings for, like, sixty dollars. We all get a good laugh out of that. I throw him a packet of pretzels from the plane, and he looks like he is gonna cry.

Brockton, Wareham, Bourne (Bourne Bridge photo with The Boys. Life's about moments in time with the people you love. Remember that), North Falmouth, Falmouth, East Falmouth, Mashpee (Good walk around the Mashpee Commons), then boom, Hyannis.

Check into the Sea Coast Inn. Frank Thomas is already wasted. He's got a fistful of Nugenix, and he is ready to clown. I was not served (our flight attendant's husband shot himself in the head when he saw the flying demons, and she blames me), but Sammo ordered for me, so I'm shitfaced as well. Sammo is sober because they thought he drank all the drinks he ordered and cut him off. Scary Mask made a prison wine, and it's hard to tell if he is drunk or very ill.

Our big thing is cutting costs, so we get one room. Sammo and I bed together because he is mega respectful, and if we bump legs, he doesn't have leg hair, so it doesn't freak me out.

We take our shit up to the room. We haven't even set our bags down, and Frank Thomas is calling for shots. Crazy bastard. We're all pretty old now, so when I pour everyone a shot of Kahlua, we aren't downing it right away. We're sipping it, but it's all good because The Boys are together again.

Couple things get brought up. Sammo asks why I am 100 pounds. I appreciate this question because I get to tell my friends I banged a chick! I tell them. Definitely get high fives, but not super strong high fives? I think I might have confused them when I said all the stuff about other universes and how we are the two people on the dividing line of good and evil. The flying demons don't ever tell the full story. Sound like anyone you know?

Scary Mask says, well we are more concerned that you had sex with a woman and now you look really sick. And I'm like, "Oh, do you wanna change my diapey? Are you my mommy?"

Everybody busts up. The Boys are back.

They ask about Lucifer's Champion. I'm like, "Give it a rest. I wanna hang out, get some meat on me, and then I'll take care of him later." Sammo offers to train me in Kung Fu. I tell him, "Thanks, but no thanks. I'm here to party. Besides, this isn't a movie where I play Jackie Chan's fat friend. I'm the main guy. So, if I'm learning anything,

I'm learning Drunken Boxing." I say all of this out loud to set healthy boundaries. Sammo doesn't talk for twenty minutes, but we do another round of shots and let him walk my very clear insult off, and he's back to being my second favorite guy here.

We rush out the door because the JFK Cape Cod Museum closes at 4 PM. Cape tradition: Shots, then JFK Cape Cod Museum. It puts you in the right mindset for the weekend. You walk inside the shrine of THE Massachusetts Sex-with-Women King. You take a tame, guided tour through his life, but you and your boys fill in the gaps of what your tour guide is too afraid to tell you. Every inch of The Cape has been worn out by JFK, so when you come to lay pipe, you're standing on the shoulders of a sexed-out giant.

God, it's good to be back. I can tell The Boys feel the same way.

We get to the museum and get thrown in a private tour. Our tour guide is Derek, and he seems like he's going to be a wet blanket. He keeps trying to get us to look at Robert F. Kennedy's "Ripple of Hope" exhibit, and I'm like, fuck off. I didn't take a red-eye from San Diego to Boston to see some big-toothed second-fiddle amateur. We're here for the big guns.

Enough of this shit: I give Derek a million dollars. But I do it in a way that's meant to be demeaning. I pull his pants down and try to slip him the cash under his ball sack, but God, this kid is hung like a bull. Wild stuff.

I tell Derek to quit fucking around and show us something that's going to knock our socks off. Derek smiles like a freaking weirdo.

"Right this way," he says. What a creep.

Derek takes us from the main hall towards the gift shop. We're like, bro, we've been to the JFK gift shop. We run trains on this gift shop. He ignores us.

The JFK museum has got these beautiful colonial windows all over it. Great stuff. You can really take in Hyannis. Well, in one of these windows, I feel like someone is looking at me. When I turn around, I hear a noise of something scurrying away. So I'm being watched. Great.

We follow Derek to a shirt section. All the shirts are hung up on those circular racks that kids like to hide in. Derek looks back at us like we're supposed to be excited about shirts. Try harder, Derek.

Then he pulls apart a couple Medium shirts and climbs inside the rack. He completely disappears. I make Scary Mask reach his hand in. No Derek.

I force Scary Mask to put his body in the shirt rack. After some fighting, I give him three dollars and he jumps in, no problem. He's gone.

"Get down here boys!" We hear Scary Mask call from what sounds like fifty feet down.

Scary Mask sounds happy, and not dead, so we follow.

Fourteen

I almost lose my footing because as soon as you step in the shirt rack, you're standing on top of a spiral staircase. It's old. Frank Thomas is afraid he is going to break the thing, but Derek says that David Ortiz comes here twice a week, so Frank should be fine. Sammo moves with the grace of a leopard, so he raises no concerns. Scary Mask is down at the bottom of the staircase trying to get lendingclub.com on his phone so he can secure a high-interest same-day loan to cover the rest of this trip. Crazy bastard.

We go down the staircase. The walls are all old and brick, and the ground is packed dirt. Derek says this is what it was like back in the 1700s, and I'm like, oh, fuck yeah. We're all handed torches. Immediately, we set Scary Mask's shirt on fire. He's rolling around saying this is his last shirt, and we're like, "You said this last time we burned your shirt."

Derek waits until Scary Mask puts his shirt out, and we continue walking down the hall. We get to a door that looks fancier than anything else in this hall. Derek removes a small plastic cover next to the door that is covering some type of keypad. He punches in a code. A bunch of loud noises. Air shoots out of the door. It opens.

There is an old film projector. Next to it are some film reels covered in gold. Four soft chairs. To the left is an open bar that Derek quickly gets behind.

"Please, grab yourself a drink and make yourself comfortable. The film will begin whenever you are ready."

We all get Kahluas on ice and find our seats. Next to my seat is a hand towel with my initials on it. I feel a little titter in my body. I have ideas, but I don't want to get my hopes up.

We are all seated. Derek grabs one of the film reels and sets it all up. He turns the thing on. Me and the boys cannot believe what we are seeing.

JFK.

Laying.

Pipe.

The camera is real tight on JFK, so we get a good look at how he strokes it. Dick hangs pretty nice. Not as big as I thought, but it's got a distinctive curve to it, so you know he is hitting everything right. Son of Massachusetts slinging his wood. We are soaking in every intimate detail: the way his eyes move over whomever he is fucking. His little grunts that sound weird because of his accent. His lean body—skinny, but tastefully jacked—covered in a deep film of sweat. And, I'm trying not to be rude, but the women are orgasming big time. And these weren't any seven-second grainy clips. The film was high res and went on for two hours. JFK banging everyone you ever suspected he banged. And on top of that, he's doing all this banging with a Cape Cod backdrop. That right there makes the lion's share of my penis blood: you know JFK is loose in these videos. He's not some DC working stiff president. He's home. The kid is slinging wood in his home.

I think we all realized what the hand towels were for :)

The hand towels were for catching our cum. And cum they caught. We wipe up and grab another Kahlua. Apparently, we have to stay until the movie ends. Honestly, once we came, we felt kind of gross watching this video. I mean, this man was murdered. And now he's like, what, some fuck-horse for billionaires like me to jack off over? Jesus.

The movie finally stops. We finish our Kahluas and follow Derek out of the room, down the hallway, and up the staircase. We all shake his hand, with our jerk-off hands. Derek does not mind in the slightest. I say thanks to him.

"Anything for the Moral Center," he says, like a creep.

"Huh?"

"Many people around here, I'm sure back home as well, don't look upon you favorably. But some of us, well..." Derek smiles a big fat creep kind of smile. "...some of us are invested in Earth getting a little darker."

Ah, fuck. I just realized that getting poon on this trip might be hard because I am partly responsible for thousands of deaths. Frank offers me a bunch of Nugenix so I can grow a mustache real quick, but I turn him down. There isn't enough testosterone in the world to make that happen.

Fifteen

We go back to the hotel to freshen up for dinner. Sammo wants to talk to me out on the patio, so I follow him out there. Frank Thomas is taking a shower. Scary Mask is cutting holes in one of the pillowcases to make himself a little shirt.

Sammo closes the patio door behind us and sits down looking at a beautiful sunset. I understand things are a little dicey right now, but when the sun sets during a blood red demonic sky, it's a really fantastic color palette.

Sammo looks serious. He turns to me.

"A warrior is just that—a warrior. Greg, you can rest. Take this time to rest. But you are a warrior. It has not been thrust upon you. It is in your blood. And a warrior must fight. There is no other way for a warrior. To refuse to fight would bring dishonor."

I take it all in.

"Hey Sammo, in that movie *My Lucky Stars*, wasn't it your idea to have that scene where all the guys try to have non-consensual sex with that woman?"

Sammo laughs. He's like, "What the fuck am I even saying to you, let's tear this town up until we cum blood." We do our secret handshake, and we head back inside.

Frank Thomas and Scary Mask are in bed practicing kisses. I run up and shake the bed, like, "Come on bros! Why practice when you can have the real thing?" I give them a ten-minute deadline. I got reservations at Spanky's Clam Shack and Seaside Saloon. I've generated a good rapport with Spanky's, and I don't want to fuck that up because Frank Thomas is trying to teach Scary Mask how to bite a lip a little bit during French kissing.

Sixteen

We make it to Spanky's on time, thank God. I see Freddie Jambon is still running the host booth. Freddie is a dumpy guy in his mid-40s who I consider family. I still remember Freddie's first day. He just lost his job during the recession, and basically, this was the last place he could find work. Anyway, he lost his home, his family, real sad sack stuff. But he became a pretty good host. Never was able to go back to a regular job, so he's still here. Lives at the restaurant. The guy's a fucking animal.

Freddie sees me. Usually, Freddie runs up and hugs me and asks me if I got any job leads. This time, though, he seems a little standoffish. No hug. Which is too bad. In the Lyft over, I was telling the guys that I was going to give Freddie five million dollars if he hugged me. Let that be a lesson.

I walk up to Freddie. He's got tears in his eyes. He's shaking. He's like, "Greg, you piece of shit." Oh boy. He continues.

"My family was in Nebraska. My family is DEAD because of you. Where the fuck were you?"

I don't typically have this relationship with Freddie, but he asked, so I tell him in great detail about my sex session with Xandra. Freddie is saying things like, "You bastard," and "I would give anything to hold my wife again." The Xandra sex story is normally better when everyone hearing it has not lost a loved one recently. I wrap the story up, and I ask Freddie if he can bring us to our seats. He tells me we are no longer welcome here. Me and the boys are no longer welcome at Spanky's? What a nightmare. We dump Freddie into a trashcan and take off.

Here's what sucks though: NO ONE is letting us eat at their restaurant. Everyone has family in Nebraska, apparently. I'm getting tired retelling my Xandra story when people ask where I was when they needed me most. I'm in a bad mood. We end up going to a gas station off the rotary for hotdogs. We're bumming out big time.

I'm outside eating my four hotdogs. I hear something in the bushes. I got no time for this shit.

"Come out and say what you need to say!"

Doug and his rabbit and gopher friends come out of the bushes. I ask Doug how he got to Hyannis. He said he flew. I ask him if he went Logan or Barnstable.

Doug went Barnstable. I tell him he did it wrong. Doug shrugs. He knows I'm right, but he's such a smug prick.

He stares at me with those big judgy eyes. "Greg, you're letting your world crumble," he says. I say no, I let Nebraska crumble. Insane difference. Does no one agree? Nebraska. Name your favorite thing to do in Nebraska. Who does high school and college and says, "You know where I want to end up? Nebraska."

"Greg," Doug starts to walk away from me. He faces towards the red moon. "Is death the only thing you consider destruction? Is that the only figure you use to measure the pain caused on humanity?"

I'm not, like, walking around measuring pain, Doug. What the fuck does this asshole think I do all day?

"I'm taking a break. I just fucked for fifteen years. I'm tired. My pubic bone is completely shattered. I am emaciated. Let me eat my hot dogs and have some laughs with my friends."

"You saw Xandra?" Doug asks.

"No, I fucked somebody else for fifteen years. Come on, Doug."

"Did you align your Beam Capsule to her energy force?" Doug asks. His eyes are big, trembling, black marbles. Doug is adorable.

"Doug, I fucked. If that's what you are asking, that's what I did. And she came. She said she was close, which means she did cum."

"Greg, where is your Beam Capsule?"

"Above my balls, Doug." I pull my hog out and show it to Doug and his friends. Doug shakes his head. He is mad. The other ones are clearly thinking about their own hogs and how they match up.

"Greg, where is the Beam Capsule I gave you?"

"Doug, what the FUCK is a Beam Capsule? You gave me a binder of animals. You gave me a SECOND-RATE IMAX presentation. You gave me a seafoam green gas station dick pill."

"ZQUARTOG. I GAVE YOU NO GAS STATION DICK PILL. I GAVE YOU A CAPSULE SALAVAGED FROM THE PORTAL BEAMS THAT CONNECTED THE OTHER 38 UNIVERSES TO THIS ONE. IF YOU AND XANDRA CONNECTED ENERGY FORCES, IT WOULD HAVE PROVIDED YOU STRENGTH WORTH 39 LIFETIMES. THAT STRENGTH WOULD HAVE BEEN MORE THAN ENOUGH TO DEFEAT LUCIFER'S CHAMPION."

"OKAY, DOUG? THE BEAM CAPSULE LOOKED LIKE A GAS STATION SEX PILL. SO I TOOK IT BEFORE I HAD SEX WITH XANDRA. IT MAKES SENSE WHY I WAS ABLE TO MAINTAIN AN ERECTION FOR 15 YEARS. YOU SHOULD HAVE TOLD ME—"

"I FUCKING TOLD YOU THIS, ZQUARTOG, AND YOU CLEARLY WEREN'T PAYING ATTENTION."

"THEN YOU SHOULD HAVE HAD A POST-TRAINING QUIZ, YOU LITTLE PIECE OF SHIT."

I take one of my gas station hot dogs and full-strength hurl it at his head. It bounces of his head, and he is totally fine because I threw a hot dog. But we are both steaming.

Doug doesn't say anything. I don't say anything. But I can tell we both needed that. We both needed to scream at each other. It's just something alpha, rock-star types need to do.

"Greg, I'd like to show you something. You can bring your hot dogs."

Doug puts out his paw to take my hand. I'm like, put your paw back. I'm not going to crawl on my knees just so you can hold my hand and take me somewhere. Get off your weird power trip.

I follow Doug into the bush he and his friends came out of. In the bush is a spiral staircase. I'm like, "Are you taking me to the JFK place? Because the JFK place has a staircase like this." Doug is like, "I'm not taking you to see some weird sex thing. I can't believe you did that." I roll my eyes.

Seventeen

We go down the staircase. The walls are illuminated by fireflies and glow worms. Bats come off the ceiling and fly up the stairs and outside. Doug leads me down the hallway. We are walking down this hall, and the occasional animal passing by bows at Doug. First couple bows I thought were for me, but it became clear the bows were not for me.

The hallway eventually widened and spit out to this underground metropolis built by animals. Endless skyscrapers made of dirt and trash. Neon signs reconfigured and mashed together to create new words. All the Segways that used to be everywhere are now down here, with the animals.

I want myself to have a breathtaking moment, but I can't. Honestly? The place has a terrible vibe. All the animals I see are in a bad mood. And, not to make it all about me, but it seems like every single one of them has a problem with me.

Detroit. Yeah. It's like if Detroit, was made out of dirt. Detroit used to be great. Now it's not. That's a perfect description. And, the last time I was in Detroit, a lot of people were mean to me. Major Detroit energy from this place. Totally sucks.

Doug, his buddies, and I make our way down to the city streets. Animals are bumping into me and calling me an asshole. My feelings get hurt, so I punch an orange cat in the head, and—I dunno—I might have killed that cat. Doug is turning a major blind eye due to the fact that we might have had a breakthrough. Doug doesn't know this, but I don't think we did.

Surrounding Animal Detroit are these giant—God, how do you say this—voids? Like big, black circles. And, if I'm guessing, I'd say there are 38 of them. I ask Doug about the voids.

"Those aren't voids. They are the remnants of portals. To the other universes."

"They seem dark and out of service—what happened?" I ask. Doug looks at me like our breakthrough and my safety are at jeopardy. I think for a second. Okay. Wait. Got it.

I'm the reason the portals to the other universes are dark and out of service.

Doug takes me down some dirt stairs to this monument in the center of the town. The monument is comprised of these giant granite blocks with little etches all over. At the base are some flowers and acorns and shit. Some animals are touching the blocks and crying.

"This looks like shit. What is it?" I ask.

"When you went into hiding, the war began. These are the animals that died for your cause. We honor them."

I count the names. "There's, like, more than fifty names here," I say. Doug says there are 150,000 names, so we are both right. My buzz is killed. But I'm also super understanding now. All these animals died, and the ones that didn't said, "We gotta get a block and write their names on it." And they did that. And now I'm looking at it. This is some heavy shit, and I am fully comprehending. I close my eyes to say a prayer. No words are in my brain. I fight for them. Nothing. I have nothing for these dead animals.

But I get it. It's a huge moment, and I'm proud to be a part of it. I tell Doug and the other animals that, yeah, I get it. "A lot of your friends and family died. And it probably sucked for you, and them, and others. War can be a lot of fun to think about, but a lot of war is actually bad. So I'm gonna try and end that war—"

Lots of animals start cheering.

"—in two to three days."

The cheering quiets down pretty quickly.

"A party weekend is a party weekend. Tickets can't be canceled and scheduled for an earlier flight without a serious penalty. I can stretch the weekend, though, and go on standby. I don't want to do that because standby sucks. I'd rather be on this stone block than on standby. "

My joke is not funny to this group of animals.

"Okay, so, good. To be clear: keeping my weekend plans. May extend, depending on how the weekend is going. But definitely NOT shortening the trip, because, you know, the penalties."

Doug looks at the angry crowd, then back at me. "Are you serious? You're still going to party?"

And I'm like, "You thought I was going to hop on a plane and fight without having a couple nights out with The Boys? Like, I get it, a lot of animals died, and that bums me out. But I'm also the guy who left his family to go fuck a Souplantation employee. My real wife has descended into madness, and I am unmoved."

Doug is like, "How are you at the center of the moral spectrum of humanity?"

I'm like, "It's a big fucking world, my guy."I ask Doug if there is a bathroom, and he says you can't use the bathroom, and I'm like, "Oh, so there is a bathroom," and he's like, "We should go because some of these animals are ready to kill you." Fine. I can take a hint.

Eighteen

We leave Animal Detroit and go back to the gas station. Doug stops me before I go back to The Boys.

"Greg, I'm sorry for not letting you use our bathroom. That was childish of me. I'm just—frustrated. I just thought this—you—would be different. I thought this would mean more to you. I mean, the other 38 times, it didn't mean anything to you, but I thought maybe this being the last one…Alas."

Doug is bummed. I sit on the curb so I can be on his level.

"Look, Doug. I know that fighting this guy is my job. I get that. But, it's just my job, you know? It's just another stupid thing on my list. So, I'm sorry that I'm not some great warrior that gives everyone hugs and kisses and makes cool speeches. I'm just a guy with a couple billion dollars and pockets filled with Nugenix and extra thin condoms."

Doug's shoulders tense. Man. I'm starting to notice the differences in animals, especially rabbits, and Doug looks like shit. I punch Doug on the arm.

"Doug, you party?"

Doug sighs, he says he used to fuck around before all this shit started. "Nothing too hardcore."

I'm like, "You want to come out with my boys and me?"

He's like, "Well, if you're not going back to Rancho Bernardo, then I guess." I punch Doug on the arm again—alright!

"Can my boys come too?" Doug asks.

I'm like, "Kinda tough as it is with the ratio right now. We're gonna be trying to roll into clubs with eight dudes? That's tough."

Doug's like, "We're all gay."

And I'm like, "Okay, so I tell the bouncer don't worry, half of our group will be trying to fuck each other," and Doug and I both laugh. I am laughing harder than Doug, but we're both laughing. I tell him, "Okay, go get your boys."

He grabs his boys. I grab mine. We all meet back up in the hot dog parking lot.

His boys are the two other rabbits and the gopher. I line up my boys and Doug lines up his boys.

I go first, starting best to last. "Frank Thomas, Sammo Hung, Scary Mask." Everyone nods. Doug goes next. He goes fat rabbit with floppy ears, jack rabbit, and then gopher.

"Frank, Pete, Braylen."

Bad start. Two Franks? Untenable. Doug's crew is the away team, so Doug's Frank needs to make the switch. He settles on Rudy.

But when one crisis gets settled, another one pops up. Sammo keeps asking Braylen if his name is Brayleigh. Braylen keeps saying no, but then he asks Sammo why and Sammo says he used to date a girl named Brayleigh. Now, I know that Sammo did not date a girl named Brayleigh, so what kind of shit is he trying to pull?

Doug is like, "Hey Braylen doesn't need to change his name. Sammo needs to cool it," and I totally agree. But I can't show it. Why? Sammo is my boy. So I'm just like, "I'll call a Lyft."

My boys are looking at me like, *is this a good move?*

Truthfully, I don't know.

Nineteen

There is only one place my boys and I go if we want to have a full throwdown party: Trader Ed's. DJ till 1AM. Frozen Drinks. Outside dancing. We load up on alcoholic slushies and dance the night away. Real hardcore stuff.

On the Lyft over, The Boys and I can't stop arguing about which slushie to have first. If you couldn't see the childlike wonder in our eyes, you would think it was getting pretty heated. Doug and his boys are looking at us all crazy. The tension is still high, and it doesn't feel ready to let up.

Rudy pulls out a baggie of something. The Lyft tension changes to Lyft curiosity. Rudy dabs his paw in the baggie and then sniffs his paw. He passes the bag around to his boys. I can tell Rudy is hesitant to pass the baggie to my boys or me. We're also hesitant. Sammo mouths to Frank Thomas, "Is that cocaine?" and Frank nods his head. By then, the baggie is down to Braylen. Braylen does a bump and hands it back to Rudy. Rudy looks at us and the baggie. Doug gives him a look like, "Give it up, bro."

He hands the bag to Scary Mask, and boom, it's like a fucking peace pipe. Everyone is doing bumps and having a good time, including me, because I also do some cocaine. We're like old friends. A clutch move by Rudy to somehow have cocaine, and to whip it out in public. You never know how cocaine is going to land.

We get to Trader Ed's. They don't want to let us in either. But you know what? That's too damn bad. We are eight tight bros on cocaine. We are a self-made key to the city. Frank palms the bouncer's head and threatens to Game-of-Thrones" him. Game-of-Thrones-ing someone is when you stick your thumbs into a person's eyes and reveal the truth to a suspicion they've had, just before smashing their head into the ground. We call it Game-of-Thrones-ing because this happens in the HBO Series *Game of Thrones*. It's a pretty famous part of the show, but some people haven't watched the show, so sometimes you have to explain it.

But this bouncer has seen *Game of Thrones*, and he does not want to get Red Vipered. Sometimes we call it getting Red Vipered because the guy who gets his head smashed went by "The Red Viper". It can be a lot of explanation if they haven't seen *Game of Thrones*. I've actually said to Frank that he may not even need to explain it; he normally has his fingers in the guy's eye sockets. And, I don't know, if you put your fingers in my eye sockets and then asked me to recall something from a TV show, I might forget a few plot points.

None of this matters. The bouncer lets us in.

Every conversation is super interesting, and everybody I am with is a fucking genius. I am so happy that I am not in Rancho Bernardo because I would get done with that bleeding tower too quickly. My face feels like a roller coaster, but I am also the CEO of everything sophisticated. I follow Doug into the bathroom because I don't want this feeling to end.

He sets up three lines and does all of them. Doug looks at me and is like, "How do you think I tore that coyote in half?" Then he gives me this big smile. Doug is funny as fuck! I do a little bump and head back out.

Frank Thomas has eight slushies in his big strong arms, and I have never met someone so thoughtful or pure. When Frank drops the drinks, I whisper in his ear, "In another life," and bite my bottom lip.

He stares at me with his big cocaine eyes and winks three times. I down my slushie. The brain freeze is pretty intense, and it knocks me to the floor. When I get back up, Sammo says, "Was it your scar? Is Voldemort coming?" Good one, Sammo. I unbutton two buttons on my shirt and head out to the dance floor.

Very quickly, here are my rules on dancing. Stick to the choreography. No improvisation. I have four dances that match popular music time signatures. If the song has a weird time signature, I get off the dance floor. Next, the dance floor is a place to attract women, not meet women. Do not attempt to integrate women into your dancing. If they are impressed by your dancing, they will find you off the dance floor. Last, clap for your DJ. They are up there working their tail off. After every song, clap. Don't be that guy who doesn't clap for his DJ.

Me and The Boys are dancing our asses off. The animals are bouncing from the bathroom to the bar. They dance for a couple of songs, but I can tell it's not their thing.

Naturally, I get off the dance floor for a slushie, and I got girls hounding me.

"I already came from your dancing, so don't worry about getting me off tonight,"

"I'll kill myself if I don't have you."

"I can give my boyfriend triple his dose of Zoloft so he won't hear us make love."

Shit like that. I'm trying to work my moves on them, but my phone keeps buzzing. Finally, I have to stop these women from talking so I can look at my phone.

Xandra. Shit. I head over to the balcony where I can see the boats resting on the cape, and I pick up the phone.

"Hey."

"Hey," Xandra says. "I just got off my night shift. I—" She coughs. "—I miss you."

Just those words get my thighs sweaty. "I'm in Hyannis with The Boys. I'm back in Rancho Bernardo in a couple days."

I hear some noises on the other end of the phone. If I had to guess, I think she took the phone and rubbed it against her vagina.

"Can you hear the sound my vagina just made? I want you now."

Shit. A fork in the road, and I don't know what to do. It's a Bro's Weekend! Never in a million years would I think of abandoning The Boys, or worse, bringing a girl on the trip with us. But I could feel the blood swell around my dick. My legs go numb. A voice was whispering in my head, *you deserve this.*

And that's really all I needed to hear. I tell Xandra to pack a bag and head to the Palomar Airport. I call a charter flight service and strong arm them into taking Xandra to Barnstable. I wish she could fly into Logan. Another time.

I hang up with Xandra. I feel the blood cool from my penis and go back down to my feet. I can walk again. I know what I have to do. Another rule of the dance floor that applies to life as well: always be honest with your boys.

I gather The Boys. I gather Doug's boys. God, they look like shit. Big smiles, though, so my heart feels full. I pass out another round of slushies, and I come clean.

"Boys, I invited a girl to party with us." My boys are crestfallen. Doug asks me if it's Xandra, and I say yes. Sammo asks if he can see a picture of Xandra. I show him her Facebook, and he doesn't get it. But that's not the point.

"Boys…New Boys: I have lost your trust. Let me earn it again." I smile.

"Let the cowboy do some roping." My boys come alive again. My boys know what's up! There are some boys' trips when the crew doesn't have it going on. Girls aren't digging our shit. When that happens, the cowboy has to clock in to do work. I am always the cowboy. No one else is the cowboy of the group.

Doug stops me. "If we are your boys now too, we can use some help, as well, cowboy." He gives me a bump. Man, this is going to be tough. I have never roped in animals, let alone gay animals. But with a couple slushies and a bump, I can make it work.

Twenty

I am back out on the dance floor. Shirtless. Against the rules at Trader's, but I only need an 8-count of New Radicals' "You Only Get What You Give" to make it pretty fucking clear that I am the exception. I can feel thirsty, foaming eyes on me. There is no song the DJ can throw at me that I can't knock down. I go to clap for him at the end of Harvey Dangerfield's "Flagpole Sitta," and I look up to find him clapping for me. Crazy. I am losing a ton of fluid, but I feel loose. I'm like a mother that has to lift her car because she rolled it over her baby. The Boys, old and new, are my babies.

I dance until I shut down the club. When I get off the dance floor, a multi-species crowd is waiting for me. A hedgehog in a mesh shirt approaches, but I put up my hand.

"Stop. I know you are lost in your feelings. But look towards my new boys. We are all heading to the same place. Tend to my boys, and I will reward you with the opportunity of looking at my body while I plow my soulmate."

Everybody cheers? Pretty cool. I order a couple Lyfts and head back to the place.

We get back to the hotel. Going through the lobby, I see her. Xandra, trying to book a room with a credit card she scratched the name offof. What a sneaky piece of shit. I go to the counter where she is and knock the card out of her hand.

"She'll be staying in my room."

"You said you'd only be having four people, so we charged you accordingly."

"I mean, she will not be staying at this hotel. She will leave before it is considered a full night's stay." The clerk rolls her eyes. She bought it!

Xandra looks at me. It's a mixed bag kind of look. Full sex eyes, but also some conflict. "I don't want to intrude on your party with your friends."

"Do you really care?" I said, with my dick bending against my jeans. She smiled, shaking her head no. "And besides, I think The Boys are going to be a little preoccupied."

I take her up the stairs instead of the elevator to loosen up my hammies. We walk down the hallway to the room. There's something nice about a hotel hallway. I dunno.

We get to the room. I slide the keycard in the reader very intimately. The door opens. We are knocked back by a wave of sex stink. Before I can take her hand, she takes mine and leads me into the madness.

Twenty-One

It's hard to make out who is who. Everybody is tangled up. Glad I got two queen beds instead of one king like I usually do.

I mean, right off the bat: no humans are fucking animals. I feel like I should say that. But everyone *is* fucking. The only people who are not fucking are the ones cleaning out their condoms to get back in there.

I look at Xandra. She is butt-naked, covered in baby oil. She says that she put it on during the plane ride. It smells like it, so I believe her. I pull my pants down. I'm soft. I want to be hard, but I'm soft. And it's not soft in a flirtatious way. It's blood drained. Stringy. Dull. Cocaine has ruined me. Everyone stops fucking to watch my flaccid meat dangle in the wind. I can feel the blood-forming in my pubic bone. Why won't it go down to my penis?

I hear whispers. *Is he really Earth's last hope?* I feel some of the blood from my pubic bone trickle into my buttcheeks. That's the wrong way!

Xandra smiles at me. She takes her big soft hands and slowly massages my blood pouch. She pushes it up the shaft of my penis and molds it into a great erection. She digs through her back pocket and finds a hair tie to tie off my meat.

We're good to go. I set the alarm on my phone. I don't have the bone solidarity to fuck for 15 years. Also, I'm a part of something bigger than myself, I guess.

I enter her, and she starts screaming but in a good way. I get scared because I'm not used to women making sounds when I'm the one having sex with them. She tells me everything is okay. I go back inside her. This time, I am prepared for her screaming. All The Boys including the animals trap us in this vortex of fucking. We are the eye of the storm. We hump all night and time our orgasms to the sunrise. I say something like, "I love you," and I think she says it back. We fall asleep.

Twenty-Two

I wake up six hours later. My alarm didn't go off. I guess I set my phone to stopwatch instead of alarm.

I wake up to Frank Thomas shaking me. He looks scared. His eyes are puffy and red.

"It's Doug." Frank's voice trails away. His voice never does that. I scrape Xandra's sleeping titty off my chest. Frank can't look me in the eye.

"He must have partied too hard. He's—He's not breathing." Frank takes me to the office table, which is like five feet away.

And there he is. Doug. His soft head, face down in a crazy amount of coke. His paws are lodged in the prostate of some buff looking rabbit. I can only see the back of his head, but he looks peaceful. No smugness, no sense of doom. Just a blue collar guy blowing off steam.

Brayden comes out of the bathroom with a towel around his waist. He looks at us and nods. I'm the last one to know about Doug. I ask if anyone else is in line for the shower. Apparently, Brayden was the only one who felt like it was appropriate to take a shower. Pete, Rudy, Sammo, and the other gay animals they met at Trader's are all crying and panicking out on the balcony. I can hear them talking through the glass door.

"We can't say he died like this! If our community finds out—"

"They won't."

"What do we say?"

"I'll write something. Mario. Can— hi, sweetie. Mario, can you get the hotel stationary from the nightstand?"

One of the club rabbits comes in through the glass door and grabs the stationary and a pen.

"Ok...ok. Just let me think here..."

Watching this play out gets me sad. But I'm also bored. I wake Xandra up and get dressed. Xandra and I leave the room to go get breakfast or something.

We settle on a buffet downstairs. Nice buffet. This isn't some Route 66 bullshit motel warm yogurt deal. No. Custom omelets. Six types of cereal. Bowl of fruit. Couple flavors of coffee. It's fucking king shit. 8-10 on weekdays. 10-12 on weekends. I forget what day of the week it is, but my friend is dead, so I'm going to sit in the eating area and someone is going to feed me.

But I can't even eat. I feel sick. I just, why can't I have one nice thing? Just one trip with The Boys and a nice late breakfast with my soulmate? Xandra seems sad too. She phrases it differently.

"I am sad that a kind and brave animal died of a cocaine overdose in our hotel room."

I mean, *yeah, true.*

Twenty-Three

Xandra and I go back upstairs to the room. Everyone is waiting for us. The Boys are all dressed in suits, except Scary Mask, who is in his pillowcase that he colored black. Rudy speaks.

"We must bury Doug."

"Okay," I say.

"The whole community will be in attendance."

"Fine."

"It's important that the community has an opportunity to mourn their leader."

"Hey, Rudy? You don't have to sell me on funerals."

"Ok," Rudy pauses. "You have to speak."

"Fine," I say. Rudy pulls out some stationary from one of his cute rabbit folds.

"I mean, you don't have to speak," Rudy says. He gets a look from Braylen like, *what the fuck, yes he does.*

"Well, you do have to speak, I mean. But—" He holds up the stationary. "You have to say what we wrote. It's really important."

I'm not going to bust Rudy's balls. He's got a lot on his shoulders now. I grab the stationary and throw on a suit. I put the stationary in my suitcoat. Easy day.

We put Doug in a suitcase, but we fill it with pillows to show honor. The walk from the hotel to the gas station bush is quiet. Everything looks like the end of the world, but now it feels that way, too. I wheel Doug the entire way. People wanted to take turns wheeling Doug, but what is this? What are we doing? It's a dead body. I try to avoid any cracks or speed bumps. I do a pretty good job.

Once we get to the gas station bush, and near the stairs that lead down to Animal Detroit, we line up along the spiral staircase. We pass Doug down the spiral staircase like a bucket of water. We head down the same narrow hall that people bowed to Doug at last night. We get to the end of the hall where it spits out to the Animal Detroit cityscape. The little world is waiting for us. They know he is dead, so everyone is bummed out.

A small turtle makes his way from the crowd toward me. The turtle moves faster than you would think, but it's still pretty slow. Once the turtle gets to me, it slowly unpacks a garbage bag that was resting on its back. The turtle pulls out an old toy echo microphone and hands it to me.

"Start speaking. Speak. Speak right now," the turtle says. Fuck. Fine. Okay.

I grab the stationary out of the suitcoat. I look at it. At first, I think I am still high on coke. But then I realize that Rudy and his nightclub friends wrote this shit in rabbit language. None of it makes sense. I look at Rudy and hold up the stationary. It takes a second, but Rudy gets that he fucked up. I shake my head. I don't make too big of a scene, because clearly Rudy is in over his head and you have to be tender with people that are coming down off of coke. I take a deep breath and improvise.

"Doug. I met Doug outside my bedroom window after he tore a coyote in half."

Light applause.

"I then got to talk to Doug. Wow, that guy sure liked to talk, huh?"

I pause for funeral laughter. There is no funeral laughter.

"Doug was a fighter. From what he told me, he was fighting for a lot of really good stuff. He really cared about all of you. Big time."

The turtle who was pushy a few seconds ago is now smiling.

"Doug also liked to party," I say. I hear some nervous shuffling behind me. Relax. I'm not going to say he died from coke.

"When I saw that Doug liked to party as much as me, I said 'Okay, this is a guy I want on my team.'"

Nervous applause.

"But every team, you know, has to break up," I say. Not sure if where I'm going is cool, but I feel like I can land the plane.

"The Bulls. Lakers. Patriots. The Beatles, even." I nod at what I just said. "I mean, come on. Kurt Cobain. Killed himself."

Little bit of whispering.

"I'm not saying Doug killed himself. Doug wouldn't do that. Not on purpose, at least. But you know, drugs."

The whispering is pretty loud now. The turtle, no longer smiling, comes over to me.

"Stop speaking. Right now. Put the mic in the bag. Do it. Now."

I throw the mic in the bag. I shrug at Rudy. I know I did bad, but I try and make it better by looking like I don't care. Based on Rudy's face, I'm just making it worse. Man, that got away from me.

The animals take the suitcase holding Doug down to the people. Grasshoppers are making a beautiful song as his body is taken out of the suitcase. I start to wonder if anyone will play a song for me when I die. You know what I would love? Biggest song ever played at a funeral. World record. I'd love that.

The rest of Doug's funeral is super tasteful. When they took Doug out of the suitcase, a couple of bears ate him. Tore his ass apart. But factor in the grasshopper music, The Boys in suits, and different animal culture stuff: Beautiful.

Once Doug has been fully eaten, we all head to the exit. I feel a poke at my ribs. I look down. It's a snake. Big snake. The snake is 40 feet long and now has its face next to mine. The snake speaks.

"I'm Sarah Krishna-Wallace. Doug appointed me as the head of R&D eight years ago. In that time, we made incredible strides in weaponizing recycled portal energy. We were able to make a one of a kind prototype in time for you to face Lucifer's Champion. We called it a Beam Capsule. Doug gave you the beam capsule, correct?"

"Yes," I say.

"Do you still have it?"

"Yeah it's somewhere at the hotel. Safe."

"Doug had word sent back to me that you used the Beam Capsule as a sex pill fifteen years ago."

"That is true."

"What you said before—"

"—Was a lie. I do not have the Beam Capsule."

"I see." Sarah Krishna-Wallace slithers her tongue. She sighs. "The work must go on. Sit on my back and come with me to my bungalow. Doug left something in my possession to give to you."

I sit on the Sarah Krishna-Wallace's back, and she takes me on a little choo-choo ride through the city streets. We go past the center of the city where the granite memorial is, and I see them etching one more name into the stone. We pass the city and head into a little country suburb. We find a house on a cul de sac, and Sarah Krishna-Wallace takes me up a tree and into a little treehouse. I can't begin to describe how fun the snake ride was.

Sarah Krishna-Wallace hands me a paper Vons bag. It's heavy. There is a little note taped to it. It's in rabbit, so, nice job. Useless.

I open the bag. Holy shit. It's my Cutco knives!

"While you were away, Doug retrieved these from your home. He said if we can't use the Beam Capsule, these were our next best option for fighting Lucifer's Champion." I don't know what is in that tower, but I can guarantee they have never seen a Cutco knife. I daydream about cutting a 12oz strip of porterhouse with these fucking things.

Sarah Krishna-Wallace takes me back to my friends. Again, great ride. I ask Sarah Krishna-Wallace how she pees. I don't get a firm answer.

I show my friends my Cutco knives. We go back to the hotel and order room service.

At some point during room service, Sammo says, "You look beefed out."

I look down. He's right: I'm beefed out. I'm tan. I'm ready to do damage.

Twenty-Four

The plane ride home is tense. For one, Xandra had to get the middle seat because I wasn't expecting her to be flying home with me. I got her a perfectly nice chartered jet, and she wants to huff and puff about spending time with me. I don't ask because I want to watch *The Martian*, but I think she's sad because she knows this time I am actually going into that tower. She keeps wanting to take my headphones off my head, and I keep having to tell her that I'm sharing the headphones with Sammo, so if you pull my headphones, you also pull his. Not cool. Also, this movie is super confusing, so I need to hear all the dialogue. Tricky stuff.

We land. No baggage claim, but we use the baggage claim space to say our goodbyes. All the hugs are super tender. Frank puts his big hand on my chest and says the beat of my heart is his rhythm and it always has been. So fucking beautiful. Scary Mask begs for money and doesn't understand why I won't give him any money. I give him a noogie. Good fucking people. I bow to Sammo. It's racist, but I forgot. Sammo reminds me that it is racist. I get defensive because it's more important for me to continue doing what I want than to make people feel comfortable. Tough ending to a pretty great trip, but that's how Boys' Weekends go.

Xandra and I share a Lyft. I put in a different destination than her, which gets her all misty-eyed. We hold each other for the entire ride.

Thirty minutes from the San Diego Airport to The Bleeding Tower. As much as I want to cry and scream about potentially never seeing my soulmate again, we really beat some near-rush hour traffic, so I can't complain.

We pull up to the Bleeding Tower. Still bleeding, looking like a whole bunch of shit. I get my bag out of the trunk. When I cross around the car, there is Xandra, sticking her head out of the car. She wants one last kiss. I'm like, *I pay for the Lyft, now I give the Lyft driver a show?* Jesus. I give her three powerful, irritable mouth kisses. I tell her she is more than half of me, that a universe without her makes no sense. I'm just trying to get her out of my hair so I can stretch a little bit, but apparently, she found that very sweet. She is leaking big, wet tears. But I gotta go. I slap the car. The Lyft driver says don't slap my car. I tell the Lyft driver he should go then. He goes.

Now it's just me and this stupid thing.

Twenty-Five

I hear that big stupid voice again.

"GREG—"

Shut up a second.

I look for my Cutco knives. I open the front zipper of my suitcase. Ok, I found my Cutco knives. *What?*

"ARE YOU PREPARED TO FACE—"

Enough. I am here, you schmuck. Open the goddamn door.

The door opens. Blood falling off the tower slaps the ground where the door used to be. What a mess. I enter.

Twenty-Six

I'm in the tower. It's not a super welcoming entrance. The door opened and I walked in, and I am immediately in an elevator. The transition from outside to inside is alarming. This place needs a front door, and a greeting space. Outside to elevator? Insane.

It's not a good elevator. Fluorescent bulbs in the ceiling. Everything is metal. Buttons look worn out.

I take a good look at these buttons. Ground floor has a little star next to it. Then there are numbers one through nine. Then a button that says R. No basement floor. No emergency button. No door close, or door open buttons. What a mess. And, Jesus, the buttons are all scratched up—

"—If the buttons are scratched, it's from you. You're the only one whose been in there. If you don't like it, cut your nails." I hear this from over the top of my head. I look up. In the corner of the elevator is a 12" TV monitor. The monitor flickers. It turns on.

I'm looking right at Lucifer's Champion's face. Better looking than I thought he would be. Frustrating.

"Hi," I say. I didn't want to say hi, but I was caught off guard.

"If simple pleasantries are too much for you to master, I believe this tower will make short work of you," Lucifer's Champion says with a big, fat smile.

"Hey, you know what? No more thought reading. I let it slide because I didn't want to yell, but now we have this whole electronics system set up so let's just talk with mouths. I'm at a real disadvantage if you are thought reading. I have concepts and strategies, and if I can't think about them, it defeats their purpose."

"I promise you NOTHING." The fluorescent bulbs rattle. "This is not a game, this is combat between champions of Earth and Hell. I was blessed by my King with powerful gifts. Gifts to destroy you—"

I press G for ground floor. The door opens to the parking lot.

"What are you doing?" Lucifer's Champion asks me.

"I'm going home."

"You can't!"

"No, guy, I can. If I couldn't leave, there wouldn't be a ground floor button. So, I'm going to leave, and if you want to play fair, send one of your bonobos—"

"—They're not bonobos."

"OKAY THEN WHAT ARE THEY." I take a deep breath, "It doesn't matter. Send one of your people to come get me and we'll try again."

"Greg, you dare leave—"

"—stop it. Stop pretending I'm something I'm not. Do I dare what? To leave Iowa hanging? Of course I dare. You're going up against the middle of morality. Am I going to personally walk around Iowa with a flamethrower and torch the place? No. But am I going to save Iowa and breastfeed all their children and pay off all their houses? Absolutely not. I'm right in the middle, and to me, the middle would be perfectly fine turning a blind eye to Iowa's complete destruction. I'm here because I'm properly beefed out, and I'd like to get this over with. That's it. But I can wait. If things aren't fair, I can wait. Can you?"

Lucifer's Champion shifts a little.

"You want this too bad," I say. "That's the problem with being too much of one thing. You want stuff too much. You need me to do this tower stuff. I don't need it. I mean, yeah, at some point I probably should do the tower stuff. But like if you asked me, like, 'Hey Greg, is this your dream—'"

"—I get it," Lucifer's Champion says. "Just, close the door. Okay?"

I think about it. Fine. I close the door.

"We'll talk normal. Mouths and ears," Lucifer's Champion says.

"Okay," I respond. "So what now?"

"Now, Greg Maxwell. You begin your ascent. To reach me, you must climb through your nine circles of Hell. Each floor will test your ability to overcome your vices, your demons, your—"

"—Where are you? Which button," I ask.

"I'll be waiting for you on the roof."

"Is that R?"

"Yes."

"Okay, what if I press R?"

"You can't press R until you complete your circles of Hell."

I press R. I feel the elevator move.

"HEY." I see Lucifer's Champion jump off camera. The elevator jerks to a stop.

"GREG MAXWELL, YOU CAN'T PRESS R. There are FLOORS you have to do. And you have to do ALL of them. If you press R, I won't let the doors open and you'll be stuck."

He lets out a sigh. He goes off camera for a bit. The elevator goes back down.

Lucifer's Champion is looking pretty stupid. Of course I could press R. But he got me with not opening the door. Nothing I can do about that.

The elevator stops. "Do you know what you need to do?" Lucifer's Champion asks me.

"I mean, I guess. I'm going to press a button—"

"—You are going to press buttons in order."

"Right. I press a button, and the door is going to open and—what? There's going to be some type of Hell?"

"A personal Hell for you."

"Great. And I'm supposed to, what, live there?"

"No. If you live there, that means you lost. That's your Hell now. You would be in Hell."

"Okay, so I'm supposed to not live there. Am I supposed to, like—"

"—Greg, I'm going to stop you, because I've had enough of this. Each floor is a different circle of Hell that deals with a different Torment. Your job is to overcome the Torment. If you overcome the Torment, you leave that circle of Hell. If you cannot overcome the Torment, you stay in that circle of Hell."

"How will I know what the Torment is?"

Lucifer's Champion is smiling again. "You'll know because it will torment you."

Stupid. I roll my eyes. Okay. I guess it's time to roll. I walk over to the floor buttons.

I press the "1" button. When I press the button, it changes color from white to red. The number goes away, and itis replaced with the word "Treachery". The elevator rumbles. It stops. The door opens. There is a big flash of light that consumes me.

Twenty-Seven

I am walking out of 24Hr fitness, and I feel great. Bulked up nice in the shoulders. I turn to a mirror and let myself drink my own body in. Damn. Shoulders have that little muscle that looks like a ball, and mine is popping out like a goddamn softball. What a pump. I'm thick in all the right places, and there is still a little daylight out to take this body on a little joy ride.

I make a hard left out of the gym to get some Jamba in me. My body is being patient, but I can tell it's needing an internal hose down of protein, pronto. No protein, no permanent pump. I don't make the rules.

I'm excited to see the Jamba lacrosse boys. It'll feel good to get a quick power nap on the dog bed, and maybe when we do secret handshakes they won't slap me across the face too hard.

I get to the door of Jamba Juice. I see my lacrosse boys in the window. Something's off. They don't have their usual glow of dickhead sexiness. They look scared.

I open the door, and the little bell chimes. The little bell chime freaks the boys out. Jesus.

"Sorry, Mr. Pig Girl—"

That's their name for me.

"—we ran out of protein."

I look into their narrow, sexy eyes, and I can tell this isn't another one of their little pranks. I look at the inventory in my sightline. Peanut Butter, Chocolate...all gone. Protein Powder is empty.

Okay. I mean, this is annoying, but not the end of the world. I can take a power nap on the doggy bed in the back, and when I wake up a new shipment of protein will probably be there. I'll lose some walking around daylight, which hurts.

"Do we have an ETA on that protein shipment, boys?" I ask. The tall, wiry one takes a step closer to the counter. It looks like another face is trying to come out of his face. His eyes roll back into his head.

"Never, Greg Maxwell." His body jerks around into an uncomfortable position.

"YOu'LLhaVeTogeTYouRSmOotHiEsOmEWhereElSe."

His face snaps back to normal. He looks just as scared as I feel. First, I just remembered that I am in Hell. I was fully ready to go about my life as if this was a normal place. Man. They almost got me. Second, I don't get my post-workout smoothie anywhere else. I get it at Jamba. Why? Masculine energy. It's like being in the place where the gladiators would go after a big day of killing one of their friends. Everyone is covered in blood and shit, but there is a sense of accomplishment. At Jamba Juice, it's gladiator-accomplishment shit, 24/7. It's guys being guys.

There's another place in this strip mall where a person could get a smoothie. If you can even call it "getting a smoothie."

What me and all the other rational, unemotional, middle-aged men call it is, "Getting skull-fucked by a feminist participation trophy."

The place is called Daisy's, but it might as well be called The Vagina Monologues Smoothie Company, because it practically hates guys like me and wants to see us dead. I've never been in there, but I've heard stories. And I trust these stories, because they were told by guys who are exactly like me: good, smart, and correct guys that happen to be in my

103

age group as well. Again, these are just stories, but I believe them, so they are basically true:

- First, when you open the door, they hiss at you. No "Hi, handsome." No "Oh, I've never seen such a big man order a smoothie." Just hissing.

- All the smoothies are named after Ani DiFranco songs. They don't tell you what is in the smoothie. You have to know what the song is about. It's an Ani DiFranco song, so good luck!

- If you are able to remember one song that some angry girlfriend from the past made you listen to, you can only pay in pledges for how you will positively change the community. They do not take cash. They do not take cards. You have to promise that you will volunteer.

- Finally, once your smoothie is done, they bring it out to you. But it can't be that easy. They say, "I am not serving you, because we are equals. This is an exchange of goods." Then you have to say that you are a cis white male and you apologize for being born. They say apology not accepted and dump the smoothie on your penis area. So to even get any protein, you have to rake cold smoothie off your balls into your mouth before it melts.

Again, these are just rumors. But fuck, they are probably true! My body quakes. I don't have much time. If I don't get protein in me soon, my workout will be for nothing. A day wasted.

I give my sexy Jamba Juice boys a look like, "Mr. Pig Girl is about to disappoint you." Is this me? Turning my back on my boys? I leave the Jamba Juice.

Outside Jamba Juice looks strange. Unfinished, except for the path from Jamba Juice to Daisy's. My steps don't make a sound. I hear whimpering from Jamba Juice. Every step I take towards Daisy's, the whimpering gets louder. You'd think it would get quieter. But no.

I worked hard for my body. I deserve this. I try and tell myself anything to not feel like a fucking scab.

I stand outside the window of Daisy's and look inside. Everybody in there is a woman. They are all complimenting each other and telling each other they are powerful beings that are capable of anything. *No, you're not,* I scream. What a disaster.

I open the door, and they do not acknowledge me, which is practically hissing. I freeze. The menu is a chalkboard written in cursive. I can't take this.

"I WANT A CHOCOLATE SMOOTHIE WITH PROTEIN POWDER."

The cashier's feather earrings shake from my booming voice.

"Okay, sir. We actually have multiple smoothies that have chocolate if—"

I throw a horizontal karate chop into thin air to stop the conversation. That's how women win: once they start making their point, it always appears to be better than yours. Which is why you have to just not let the point be made.

But I heard too much. Great. So she is going to make me *guess* which of these smoothies have chocolate. I can't focus. The whimpering from my Jamba boys is piercing my ears. My Jamba boys. They would never make me guess. They would tell me what I like, and feed it to me as I lay on my dog bed.

My eyes jump across the menu to the first words I recognize.

"I'll have a large, uh, 'Swan Dive.'"

"Sir, I'm sorry the 'Swan Dive' doesn't have chocolate in it. Would you like me to add—"

Okay, so now I am actually being verbally assaulted by this cashier. It's so clear what is happening that I shouldn't have to describe it. But she said with extreme clarity that every smoothie had chocolate in it, but when I choose the first smoothie I can read, I get told it doesn't have chocolate and I should go fucking kill myself?

The sheer force of her attack shoots me back against the glass door and I splatter outside. The glass door is ruined. I crawl backward crab-style to safety. I mean, now that I'm safe, I even remember her telling me as soon as I walked in that the Swan Dive ALWAYS has chocolate in it. She lied to me! Why would she lie! I try to scream something sexist, but my throat is too dry. I try to move, but the only direction I can go is back towards Daisy's. I am on my knees in the strip mall parking lot watching my body turn into bleached bones. I am no-shit dying. Fuck showing off a pump: I am actually a person who is dying.

I need the prot'. But I can't...

Can't...

My eyeballs evaporate. I am a bleached skull in a strip mall. I have lost all my gym gains, and more.

I am nothing for what feels like two, maybe three minutes. Then a light flashes.

Twenty-Eight

I wake up in the elevator to a voice. It is Lucifer's Champion. He is telling me to wake up. I tell him, "I'm up."

He's like, "I can't believe the very last circle of Hell for you is having to get a smoothie from a different smoothie store." I'm still trying to shake off that I was a pile of bones.

"Did I do good? Did I fail?" I wait. I hear a long sigh come out of the TV.

"You didn't fail. I wouldn't say you did good. But, no, you did not fail," Lucifer's Champion says.

"Damn," I say. "And you said that was the last circle of Hell? So am I done? Did you wrap all the other floors into that challenge?"

He's like, "No, you idiot, you start from the last circle and work your way up."

I'm like, "Why?"

He's like, "Did you see where you entered the tower? You entered from the bottom. I am at the top of the tower. I'm not going to have you come into the bottom of the tower, then have you ride up the elevator, then have you proceed down the levels, finish, then bring you back up to the top."

Fine. Okay. Good. That's like the first thing that has made sense. If I was in charge of this tower from a logistics perspective, I would have had it break the surface of Earth upside down. Now you got all the circles of

Hell in the right order and someone can still enter from the bottom. I keep this to myself though.

I take a seat. "Get up," Lucifer's Champion says.

"Shut up, " I say as I reach for my toes. "That was a complete shit show. I'm just supposed to roll into another circle of Hell?" I give him a look that lets him know he is stupid.

The room instantly gets super cold.

"What the fuck, man," I say.

"Did I not say I could do that? I'm sorry. Remember that I've dealt with you 38 times before this."

It's too cold to do a hammy stretch. Dangerous even. I get up. I'm butt-hurt, no question.

I press '2'. When the button is pressed in, the color changes red and the word "FRAUD" appears. The elevator shakes. It opens.

Twenty-Nine

I am in a car. I look out the window. I see a bunch of trees. I feel an island breeze. The road is very narrow. On the radio, a tape is playing. Someone is talking, and I can tell they have been talking for hours.

I know exactly where I am. I am on the Road to Hana. I must have either died, or I got accidentally put in the good room because the Road to Hana is the perfect vacation destination. Driving. Everyone has to shut up because something is on the radio. And at the end of seven hours of driving, you can get snow cones. Walt-Disney-level shit.

I'm in the front seat, but I'm not actually driving. Everything is happening for me. Also, I can only see like twenty feet ahead. Beyond twenty feet, it looks like the world has not been built yet. I see a tropical rainfall against my driver's side window. Outstanding stuff. I roll down the window, and I stick my hand out to catch some of the sweet Hawaiian rainfall. I pull my hand back. It's covered in blood. I hate this place.

My hatred goes away because my car pulls around a sharp turn and about two hundred feet away is the snow cone station. I really wish Lucifer's Champion could have done me the common courtesy of starting me at the beginning of the road. It's a seven to nine-hour drive, and I got, what, two minutes? Am I supposed to pretend I took a picture next to an ensete plant?

I pull off the road into the dirt lot next to the snow cone station. I get out of the car. I walk towards the snow cone stand.

I can't read the menu. None of the words make sense. The man behind the counter has black eyes and horns like Lucifer's Champion, but also looks like the *Moana* guy.

"Don't worry about the flavor. It'll be fine." He smiles. His teeth are rotten. A spider crawls out of a hole in a tooth. Looks like a cane spider. You're gonna see them on the Road to Hana. You can choose to freak out, or you can choose to accept that they exist. The spider creeps down his neck and across his arm. The guy stretches his arm towards me. The spider jumps off his arm and onto my neck.

I feel light spider feet, then I feel a dull pain. A jet of something hot pushes out of the spider and into my body. I stumble back. I feel drunk, but not ready to have a good time. That can only mean one thing: I have been poisoned.

I hear the snow cone guy trailing behind me. "Alright, let's have ourselves a little talk, then I'll get you that snow cone. And you are gonna want that snow cone."

I stumble over to a park bench. The snow cone man follows me. He sits on the other side of the park bench.

"I have a couple questions for you, and if you can answer them truthfully, we can get you a snow cone."

I'm like, "I'm clearly dealing with a lethal dose of spider poison. You're telling me if I answer some questions, I'll get a snow cone? Not my main priority, but, fuck it, ask the questions."

The snow cone man's eyes flash red.

"Is your name Greg Maxwell?"

"Yes." Nothing. Feel the same.

"Are you the GM of the San Diego Padres?"

"Yes. 13-time world champs." Nothing.

"Did you write the pilot for *Spartacus: Blood and Sand*."

Little backstory on this: in between baseball seasons around 2009, my wife was on a weekend memorial service thing for her grandfather. I got some screenplay software and knocked out the first season of what came to be *Spartacus: Blood and Sand*. I don't really talk about it because I'm not some guy who talks about what he did on the weekend.

But yeah, I totally wrote the first season of *Spartacus Blood and Sand*. So if I wrote the first season, I definitely wrote the pilot. So yeah. No big deal.

"Yep," I say, and—it's wild—but a tooth rips out of my mouth and lands on the table. I scream because that was not a baby tooth. That tooth was prepared to remain in my mouth for a long time. The snowcone man's eyes flash red again.

"Hmm. So *did* you write the pilot to *Spartacus: Blood and Sand?*"

Okay so, quick amendment to the story: I didn't buy screenplay software. I did it on Word, but I made it look pretty close to how a screenplay should look. But, I mean, come on: what a thing to rip my tooth out for.

I answer him again. "Well, I mean, I wrote the story so—" and another tooth rips out of my mouth. Same situation. What's funny—I mean it's not funny, I'm in a lot of pain—is I actually have a tooth that I think *could* come out, no problem. But that tooth has not been touched. This guy is clearly taking the teeth I am confident in. And to that I say: fucking stop it.

Okay, I didn't know snow cone salesmen had to go to law school so let me add another piece to my story: I got some help. I'm not some johnny-dicks-around-on-computers. I'm not a typist. I'm a dreamer. And I've got a real mind for TV. Name a show: *Breaking Bad. Entourage.* I've seen *both* of those shows.

I speak. "I wasn't the only person who wrote the script. I had a team of other people—" I don't get to finish my point because my front tooth rips out and lands next to the other two. Now I look like shit.

111

With all of these teeth getting ripped out of my mouth, I almost forgot I am also suffering internal organ damage from the poison. What a one-two punch.

"I should mention—" the snow cone man begins.

"—you should save some teeth for your snow cone. It could really cool down whatever you're feeling inside." He smiles again. This time, it's two spiders that crawl out from the cracks in his teeth. Bad news: both spiders bite me. More hot lava in my insides. What a mess. I take a swing at the snow cone man, but my hand cuts right through him.

"Greg, just answer my questions. Did you write the pilot for *Spartacus: Blood and Sand*?"

I cringe. What I think was my liver is now a puddle of spider goo. My gums are raw and bleeding.

Thank God I have 47 teeth. I grit the 44 I have left.

I mean, everything that I have said is true so far, but if I need to, you know, lay it all out there, and get into the nitty gritty of what happened, fine.

Did I get help writing *Spartacus: Blood and Sand*? Yes.

Did the people who wrote *Spartacus: Blood and Sand* know they were helping me? No.

Did the people who wrote *Spartacus: Blood and Sand* know me? No.

Do *I* know who wrote *Spartacus: Blood and Sand*? I like to think I do in some sense, but no.

Can all those things be true, and can it also be true that I wrote *Spartacus Blood and Sand*? From my perspective, of course it can, but I dunno. Everyone has their own way of looking at things.

I try and tell the story how this snow cone guy likes it. Straight facts, boring, not fun, and truthful. "I did not officially write the pilot of *Spartacus: Blood and Sand*. I saw *300* with my wife and said, 'I wish I could watch *300* forever.' Then, I saw *Spartacus: Blood and Sand* came out a few years later."

No teeth fall out. Okay! Good stuff. I smile at the snow cone guy, and he smiles back.

"I would like my snow cone now," I tell him. He keeps smiling at me, then motions a distant cloud in the sky to come closer to us. It glides to about two feet away from us. The cloud clears up a bit. When the cloud fully clears, I see Frank Thomas unpacking his bag after our Boys trip. He looks great. Real trim.

It's interesting that I'm getting shown Frank Thomas. I forgot to mention that a big part of Frank and I's friendship is based on me writing *Spartacus: Blood and Sand*. We *met* when I stumbled into the visitor's locker room and watched him shower, but that's not actually when we became *friends*. In reality, he beat the living shit out of me that day because he thought I was some sick pervert. No, our friendship kicked off because he thought it was cool that in one weekend I wrote a whole first season of a hit TV show. I think it's pretty cool I did that too. Technically, I guess, it could be argued that I didn't do that.

But whatever, I think this is interesting. I'm curious what is going to happen.

The snow cone guy's eyes flash red. Frank looks up from his tight collared shirts. He has this concerned look on his face. He runs over to his nightstand and grabs his laptop.

He heads to iMDB. He searches for *Spartacus: Blood and Sand*. I find this coincidental because I was just talking about *Spartacus: Blood and Sand*.

He searches on "Writer" for the pilot episode. Steven S. DeKnight. The guy is also tagged as the creator of the show, which is weird, because my interpretation of the facts has me creating the show after watching *300*.

Frank Thomas throws his laptop across the room. He charges around his house. He finds every picture of me—there are hundreds—and smashes them.

Jesus. Well, thank God it's just a simulation and after this—

"No, that was real," the snow cone man says. And now I'm the one flipping out.

"WHAT? ALL OF THOSE PICTURES ARE NOW RUINED?" I'm spitting tooth cavity blood everywhere.

"Greg, did you think there wouldn't be consequences for your lies?"

"THERE HAVEN'T BEEN ANY SO FAR." I can't paint it any better: everything sucks right now. I feel like shit internally, externally, and emotionally. I'm in the holy trinity of pain.

How many more of these fucking questions do we have?

"Just a few more," the snow cone man says. He pushes the old cloud away.

"Did Tony Hawk show you his secret skate park?"

"Yeah." Thank God. Back to easy questions. It's common knowledge that every San Diegan has an intimate relationship with Tony Hawk. Tony Hawk, Nick Cannon, Mario Lopez: any San Diegan has 24/7 access to them.

"Naturally," the snow cone man says. "But did you beat him in SKATE?"

Oh fuck. This guy is an animal. I can already feel the tooth he is going to pull. It's not the one I want him to pull. It's a good one. Not only that, but my skin is starting to seep hot orange liquid from the pores.

I try switching up my attack. "Please daddy, don't tell my secrets. Please, daddy. Daddy: secrets do not tell! Daddy. Daddy, please!"

No teeth rip out, but another spider pops out of his smiling face and bites me right on my goddamn eye. I can't slap the spider away because my hands are waterlogged with the orange goo. Begging did not work.

"NO, I DIDN'T BEAT HIM IN SKATE. But I was clo—" I choke on blood. The stupid cloud comes closer. It clears up. I see Frank Thomas again.

I like to think that Frank Thomas likes me for many reasons, but if I had to stick with the facts, I'd feel comfortable saying he likes me for two very specific reasons. One is that I wrote the pilot to *Spartacus: Blood and Sand.* The other is that I managed to beat San Diego legend Tony Hawk in SKATE, at his own secret skate park.

Frank is sitting in his living room. He is surrounded by broken picture frame glass. He's—well this is nice—he is actually trying to put together one of the pictures of me he broke. But, the snow cone guy's eyes flash red, and Frank Thomas is running off to his bedroom so he can get his laptop he threw.

Okay, so he's on YouTube now. He's typing in my name and Tony Hawk's name. First video that pops up is a six-minute video of me at Tony Hawk's secret skate park. Tony Hawk is trying to teach me how to drop in on a three-foot ramp, but I'm too scared. I'm crying and threatening to kill myself. Around minute five, Tony Hawk starts screaming that he wishes I would kill myself. We both look awful. The video doesn't necessarily rule out that I beat Tony Hawk in SKATE, but it makes the situation tricky.

Clearly the situation is tricky because there goes Frank Thomas, throwing his laptop and smashing photos again. He is crying so hard that he is dry heaving.

The cloud goes away. I try to tell the snow cone guy to fuck off, but nothing comes out of my mouth but orange goo and chunks of my internal organs. I want to cry, but I can't spare anything else coming out of my body.

"Last question. Do you love your stepson Ethan?"

"No." Thank god. Easy question. He gives me my snow cone, and I gobble that fucker up. I fall off the park bench, and everything goes white.

Thirty

I wake up in the elevator. I run my tongue across my teeth. All there. Maybe the Frank Thomas thing didn't happen either. I dunno. If I get out of here, I'll pretend like it didn't happen. If Frank brings it up, I'll do my best to deny it. But if he really pins me down, I'll begin the process of repairing the friendship. He's worth it.

Long pause between me and Lucifer's Champion. I look at him through the TV and give him a thumbs up sign. He kind of nods like, "Yeah, you finished."

Ok. Cool. Cool. Cool.

There's a little bit of silence. "How many teeth do you have?" Lucifer's Champion asks.

"47, not counting molars."

"Why do you not count the molars?"

"It's cheating," I say. I press number '3'. The button goes red. The word "VIOLENCE" appears.

Thirty-One

I am in a tunnel. At the end, there is light. I walk towards the light. Maybe I'm dead. Who cares. I hear sounds that I recognize. Smells, too. I keep walking.

I get to the end of the tunnel, and I look out. Great. I'm at a Padres game. So I'm at work. Fuck. This is Hell.

I look down at my hand, and a ticket appears. General plaza seating. So I am at work, but I don't even get to sit in my booth? I have to sit with general plaza people? You know what I call them during work meetings? "Poor pieces of shit." I have to say that I'm joking because everyone gets weird. Once I say that I'm joking, everyone has to laugh, or they don't have a sense of humor.

This is really upsetting, though. So in this Hell, I'm some poor piece of shit who is stuck at a baseball game? These really do get harder. I see a couple food vendors in my section, so, whatever. I go find my seat.

I find my seat. I had to push through a lot of fat slobs to get there. You know what's interesting though? No faces. I mean they had hats and double chins and clothes, but no faces. I gotta say, if you take that much time to make the person, just make the face. I sit.

I look out at the field. Fresh cut green grass. Ugh. What the fuck is this stupid sport. That's so much grass. This game takes up too much space. Baseball should be played in a hallway. Let the ball bounce off the walls. Let's have some real danger. I really feel my blood boil looking at this grass. They clearly put time into creating the grass effect with the sole purpose of upsetting me. No faces, but they really ate up the budget on grass.

The game is strange. It's clearly baseball, but it's this interpretive dance style of baseball that makes me feel like I shouldn't watch, but I should know baseball is being played. Fine. I wouldn't watch even if it was real baseball. I call over a faceless food vendor and order three hotdogs. I tell the hotdog vendor that I don't have any money because this is Hell. That's good enough for him. He leaves.

I look past the baseball game into the stands in center-right field. There's commotion. Good commotion. Some guy is trying to get a wave started. God fucking bless him. I'm all in favor of anything that takes attention away from the actual game. Fans should start waves, get in fights, throw things on the field; I'm a major advocate for mean-spirited signs. I mean, these fans come in, pay a ton of money to sit and watch a dumb game, and people like this guy take it upon themselves to make the game have a little pageantry. I tried for years to get rid of the National Anthem and replace it with a three-minute long wave. Put me on the radar for a lot of terrorist groups.

But this guy has got his section going. They are lathered up, super motivated by this guy. The wave is strong. It's working over to a couple other sections. It gets over about five sections but keeps dying at the sixth. Can't get off the ground. It's falling flat, completely out of nowhere. Well, to the untrained eye, it's out of nowhere. I start to search through the sixth section to see who is dragging us all down. There is always one prick.

I find him. Fanny pack. Glasses. An actual face. And—fuck me— he's focused on keeping score of the game. Hey, dumbass, we already keep score. It's called computers. This loser is keeping his whole section on lockdown so he can ensure that his dumb little scorebook will be accurate. What do people get from keeping score? Every team already bought a fucking scoreboard! But because YOU want to keep score, everybody else has to behave and not do The Wave? I can feel my teeth about to break.

I go back to the original section where my guy is trying to get the party started. He is visibly distraught. Again, no face, but the body language is tragic.

My heart rips open. This horrible nerd is hurting a person that I basically consider family. Normally, I would see all of this from my booth. I could then make a phone call to security and tell security to go put a gun in the nerd's mouth and demand that he put his hands up when the wave goes by. But I'm not that guy in here. I'm a poor piece of shit. I have to fight my own battles.

I get out of my seat. I head towards this bastard on the other side of the field. I don't have to shimmy my way around anyone: I am floating on this invisible bridge that goes across the baseball field and ends right next to this big nerd. Everything to the sides of me is fading away. All the focus is on this big nerd.

There are times I do leave the booth to fight fans. You get a weekday day-game, and it's practically guaranteed I am fighting a fat slob. My fighting style for baseball game environments is pretty meat-and-potatoes. No grappling, because I don't want to roll on the disgusting ground. I like a straight right punch to the throat. Normally ends pretty quickly because they think they are going to die. They're not, but it feels that way. So they roll around, someone body grabs me, and I get sent back up to the booth.

I step off the invisible bridge, and I am within arm's reach of this asshole. I hit him with a throat punch. Connects clean. In fact, he doesn't even move. But before I can throw a second throat punch, I am rocked by this crippling blow to the throat. I can hear the crunch of my windpipe.

Ok. This guy is fast. Probably took a self-defense class because he knows that he brings this violence upon himself.

I hope that self-defense class has a refund policy, because I force the pencil out of his hand and stab him in the eye. Normally I do not ramp up to attempted murder, but my throat hurts, and he should die for this.

Damn. Motherfucker. I lose sight in my left eye. I look on the ground with my right eye, and there is my left eye staring back at me. I put the eye in my pocket.

I look back up at the nerd. The nerd is not moving. I can't really grasp what is going on, so I take the invisible bridge back to my seat. Sometimes you hate to retreat. Regroup. I have lost an eye and can barely breathe. I am going to rest up, grab a hot dog, and wait this one out. I look up at the scoreboard on the way over. It's the first inning. Jesus fuck.

I can't stress enough how much it hurts to not have an eye when you very much had an eye a few seconds ago. What I think goes unappreciated is whenever wind touches my eye socket or it itches, I want to rub it. But when I go to rub it, it's just an open, fleshy eye socket. And my eye socket really itches. I try rubbing it with my hot dog, and it kind of feels better. So I make that hot dog my eye-socket hotdog, and I buy another hot dog for eating.

Also, eating with a crushed windpipe is a chore. I can't chew my hotdog enough to get through the small gap in my windpipe. I choke, and I have to vomit the chunks out.

The wave guy is even more distraught now. He clearly wanted me to win the fight. To be his champion in combat. I retreated. Every second of my retreat is a second he can't do the wave.

God, I really hate that nerd guy. I look up at the scoreboard. Still top of the first. I sit with the hotdog against my eye and think.

I am at a baseball game. There is a guy who wants to start the wave who I have developed maternal instincts for. There is a big nerd who is ruining everyone's good time. I punched him and stabbed him, and now I can't breathe, and I can't see out of one eye. He is still there. I am still here. The wave is still not getting past his section. Think.

I think. I really do some huge thinking. But I keep coming to the same conclusion: a person who stops a wave from going through their section deserves to get punched. So I get up, go over the invisible bridge, grab the nerd's new pencil and stab him in his other eye.

Boom. Eyesight lost. Did not expect that. Both of my eye sockets really hurt. I hold my hand up and scream for a hotdog. I get one for each eye socket.

I can feel that the nerd is still alive. The sound of the wave gets closer. Then it stops. Then I hear it in the distance coming closer again.

Ok. I gather my thoughts.

I have lost both of my eyes. I don't know what inning it is. The wave is not going past me. The nerd is still there.

I can't see the scoreboard anymore because my eyes are gone. The only guy who can tell me the score is the guy I want to die.

I turn towards the general direction of the nerd.

"Why can't you stop being an asshole and do the wave? You're breaking everyone's heart."

I hear a deep, clicky voice. "Keeping your own stats captures the poetry of the game." My face is hot. I'm ready to stab him again. "You know what I like to do with these stats, Greg? I take them home so my kids can do advanced stats. That's how you know who the real baseball players are."

Oh boy. I want to jump out of my skin. *Advanced* stats? Are the stats we keep not advanced enough for you? Advanced stats mean nothing. Nothing! You know what stats matter: height and weight. You find the biggest guy who says he can play baseball, and you put him on your baseball team. That's it!

I reach out into the air, hoping I grab his pencil. This time, I'm going to slit his fucking throat. Magically, I get the pencil. He graciously lets me pat up his entire body so I can find his throat. I cock my arm back to cut this fucker open. A sharp voice enters my head. A woman's voice.

"DO. NOTHING." There's a faint scream.

The voice didn't sound shrill or naggy, so I could listen pretty well. I drop the pencil. I do nothing. Now what? The wave was still not coming past us. I still can't see. This motherfucker is still keeping score for his little nerd family at home. And I'm doing nothing.

I feel like a million years go by. I ask the nerd guy what inning we're in.

"Bottom of the 2nd."

I hate baseball. But I'm doing nothing. All I can hear is the failure of a wave, the cries of the guy who wants to start the wave, and the scratching of the pencil against the paper scoreboard.

I start to count the scratches. Every scratch has to mean something right? Unless he is doodling. I wait until I hear a hundred scratches. I ask the nerd what inning we are in.

"5th"

Okay. Good. Time does, in fact, move. I order more eye socket hotdogs. I lock back into the pencil scratches.

This baseball-game-Hell-world knows I am doing well. It makes the screams of the wave man louder. He starts calling my name. He is pleading for me to help him. To kill the nerd keeping score. I want him to be strong. *Just watch the game like a big fat loser. There will be other games.* I must be strong, too.

I wait for 300 scratches this time. I ask the nerd.

"Bottom of the 6th." I am in shock.

"Padres went on a real tear. But that's just baseball."

Ooh, that little comment got to me. I flick him in his ballsack. My ballsack coils in pain. I can handle it. But I can't handle the non-linear pattern of the game. I pray for a rained-out game that I know will never come.

The screams keep growing. The only solace I take in the screams is that it must be getting closer to the end. I still feel like shit. I flick the nerd's ballsack again. I know it's going to hurt like last time, but last time, I secretly liked the pain. I grow hard in my penis. Then, I dunno: I guess I spend the rest of the time flicking this guy's ballsack. I still hear the wave guy screaming, but it's kind of getting me harder? I stop caring about what inning I'm in. My ballsack hurts so good. Damn. This nerd is helping me be a certified freak at this Padres game. I switch my flicks to two finger flicks and that blows my top off. I mush my jeans bad. I throw my head back so hard the hotdogs fall out.

When they fall out, I'm looking up at the florescent lights of the elevator.

Thirty-Two

I scream at the TV. "That one went too far!"

"I made you watch a baseball game for a regular amount of time without killing a person. All you had to do was sit and watch a game, and you almost died. The only reason you didn't die is because you learned that you like having your testicles flicked."

I mean, it's not the only reason. I also heard a little voice, but for the most part, yes. The ballsack thing was clutch. And fun.

I press '4'. It flashes red, and the word "HERESY" appears. Nothing happens.

"Just press '5'," Lucifer's Champion says.

"Why?"

"We are still working on a scenario for Heresy. There's no God, so Heresy doesn't make sense."

"If there is no God, then how is there a Hell?"

"Try not to think of them as related. There is a Hell, but there is no Heaven."

"That doesn't seem fair."

"Is there a Santa Claus?"

"No."

"But you thought there was a Santa Claus."

"Yeah."

"How did you deal with that?"

"I cried."

"Ok. There is no Heaven, Greg. Would you like to cry?"

"Fuck off." I press '5'. The button turns red. "ANGER" appears.

Thirty-Three

I am in an office room. I recognize this place. It's a building one block away from Petco Park where the Padres play. I use this place for corporate retreats or when I need a large space for telling a lot of people bad news. Last Christmas, I had to tell the entire staff that I had to throw them all in a trade to make the salaries work. It was like 148 people. All got shipped to Kansas City. And these weren't players. This is like, Debra, who hands out fliers. It's not an easy job. By that, I mean my job. Debra's job? I dunno, I think anyone can do that job. In fact, nobody has to do that job. Never filled it after Debra left. She handed out fliers. Who cares?

I am one person in a circle of people. We are all standing. Not sitting. A bunch of adults in a circle. I feel a wave of deep anger: we are about to do a corporate team-building activity.

All of my coworkers have no faces except fortwo black eyes. Everyone is wearing the same Padres polo. Even though everyone's personality is basically two dots for eyes, I can tell everyone is bummed out to be here.

A grown man in a tight plaid flannel jumps into the middle of the circle. He is clapping his hands. He doesn't tell us to clap our hands, but I can tell he wants us to clap our hands. We all look at him like he is a fucking asshole. Even in Hell, no one wants to do corporate team-building exercises.

One person in the circle claps a couple times, then stops because they are the only one who clapped and now they look like an idiot.

The plaid shirt guy gives up trying to get a clap going. "Great! In improv, that's what we call a pattern. One person does something. Then, everybody jumps in and supports!"

No one in the circle acknowledges the plaid shirt guy.

I know that I am going to have to finish this team-building exercise. In real life, I have never finished a team-building exercise. We have them every month because "Corporate Culture" is the one thing I do not have control of for the San Diego Padres. Normally, I pretend to get hurt or "get a phone call" that Ethan is dead to get out of this nonsense.

There is a timer in the corner of the room. It's ticking down from sixty. Ok. One hour. I have to do this for one hour.

The plaid shirt guy reaches into a velvet bag next to his feet. He hams up digging inside the bag. He pulls out nothing. But, oh my god, he is pretending to hold something. He tosses this pretend thing in the air and then catches it. He pretends it is heavy. There is nothing in his hand. I want to kill myself.

"We're going to play a game called Red Ball! In my hand, I have a red ball. See?"

People in the circle nod. Traitors. *No. There is nothing in your hand. You are an adult.* I say none of this out loud.

"I am going to pass the red ball to someone in the room. But before I do it, I am going to make eye contact with the person I want to throw it to and say 'red ball.' And the person who will be catching it will say 'red ball, thank you.' Then I throw the ball to that person. Sound good?"

Everyone nods their head. I look at the plaid shirt guy. He has a full face and normal eyes. From my experience on the last floor, I make a mental note not to stab this guy. He holds the fake ball up and tosses it to the person next to me.

"Oops! I forgot to say 'red ball!' I broke my own rule," he says. He gets some polite laughter. My jaw clenches.

"Oh for FUCK'S SAKE!" I can't stop myself. But I'm sorry: this man is a fucking clown. I hear a beep in the corner. I look over at the timer. The timer clicks, and one hour is added. I now have one hour and fifty-seven minutes to go. You've got to be kidding me. I can't have one outburst? This guy can't remember the rules to a child's game, but I have to be perfect?

The person throws the ball back to the plaid shirt guy. They say 'red ball' so everything is fine. The ball starts to get passed around. Some people are really making a meal out of it. Following the imaginary ball with their little bead eyes. They make the ball heavy or sticky. Real stupid shit. Nobody is bringing the house down with laughter. When the ball gets passed to me, I make a mental note that I will be the funniest one in this goddamn circle.

The ball gets passed to me, and I say, "This ball smells like my Dad's nutsack!" A lot less people laugh than I thought would.

"Greg, don't go blue. Play to the top of your intelligence," the plaid shirt guy scolds me.

Oh, fuck you. That was hilarious. I throw the ball to some fat guy.

Some short woman pipes up. "Greg didn't say 'red ball!'" Everyone laughs. I hear that beep again.

Another hour is added. Two hours and fifty minutes. Oh, so I also have to follow the rules? I can't reel it back.

"WE ONLY DO THIS TEAM-BUILDING SHIT SO SOMEONE CAN LOOK THROUGH YOUR DESKS AND COMPUTERS WHILE YOU PLAY STUPID IMAGINARY BALL GAMES." Everyone looks at me. Beep.

Another hour added. I now have one-half of a workday devoted to this shit. It's crystal clear what has to be done. I know the rules of this floor, but they are honestly perverted. Not only do I have to comply with this team-building bullshit, I have to embrace it.

Easier said than done. Plaid shirt guy pulls multiple imaginary balls out of the bag. They are all different shapes. One, apparently, is a feral cat. If you catch that one, you have to pretend like you are being mauled. I got a feral cat thrown at me six times. I am on the verge of tears with frustration. But I manage, all six times, to pretend to get mauled.

We play the next game. All of us have to pretend to be a part of something bigger. So like, a washing machine. Someone has to be the door, someone has to be a piece of clothing, whatever. I choose electrical cord for anything electrical because I can get away with lying down. I can also close my eyes and pretend it's a fun choice I am making to fall asleep. I could tell I came close to getting another hour added when someone else did electrical cord before I could. Instead of losing my shit, I said I was a surge protector and laid down next to him. When the teacher wasn't looking, I kneed this fucking asshole in the lower part of his spine. No beep.

Next is a game where we have to all hold hands and get tangled. Then we have to work together to get untangled. I started to wonder if this guy had enough material to cover the hours we had left. But I'm a terrible judge for this kind of stuff. If this class were 45 seconds, I would still think the teacher stretched everything out too much.

My first thought was, hey everyone: just go out the way you came in, but of course, the biggest fucking moron in the group has to lead us, so we stay tangled way longer than any group of adults should. I'm shaking and crying. But I'm playing along. A couple of the guys are looking at me, like, "Us three would KILL at getting untangled."

The shit keeps rolling. We play a ton of games. The two guys I bonded with become really tight with me. We absolutely crush. The teacher is getting a little jealous because it's clear that the three of us have a natural chemistry and he has no chemistry with anyone. During a break, I ask the two guys if they would want to get a three-person improv team going. Just something local, but if it pops, hey, I'd put it on the road. They say yes, because they feel the energy too. Right in the middle of exchanging numbers, everything goes white.

Thirty-Four

I wake up back in the elevator. I'm heated.

"Hey, what the fuck? How am I supposed to schedule practice if I don't have their phone numbers?"

"Those two aren't real. You beat the floor. Shut up." He clearly didn't like that I fell in love with team-building and improv.

Something's bothering me, though. "Hey, that guy running the workshop—"

"—Yes, he is a real human."

I knew it.

"Why didn't you just make an improv teacher?"

"This is Hell. You think I have to *make* an improv comedy teacher?"

Fair point. "What's the next one?" I ask.

"It should be obvious," Lucifer's Champion says.

I press '6'. The light turns red, and the word "GREED" appears. The elevator rumbles. The door opens.

Thirty-Five

No flash. No intricate destination. It's just me, a bunch of money, three wolves, and Scary Mask tied to a post. I say "hi" to Scary Mask, and he says "hi" or "please help me." I dunno. There is also a table with a letter on it. I pick up the letter.

This is your friend. He is real. You have considerable wealth, and he has none. You have two choices: give him half of your entire wealth and make him your equal, or give him none and watch him die. You leave this room either way, with a friend, or with your wealth. You can't have both.

Okay. Straight forward, but tough. I've known Scary Mask for a long time. Childhood. Had some no-shit bonding moments. But, I dunno. I think, and if I am being honest, safety nets are ruining this country. Don't look for a handout, look for a hand-up. But also, why should I give you my hand? I may need my hand.

Scary Mask can see how much this is torturing me. "Please, Greg," he says.

"Just once, Greg. Just once," He wants to say more, but he is helpless. I hate seeing my friends like this. I can't believe I'm going to do this, but I don't forget my friends.

I agree to give 10% of my wealth. That is more than enough. Too much, in my opinion. I push 10% of my wealth towards Scary Mask.

Takes a while because it's billions of dollars. Before I head back to the elevator, I make it very clear to the wolves that I am confident that the other 40% will trickle down to Scary Mask, if it hasn't already.

The wolves do eat Scary Mask. Super unfortunate, and confusing. I head back to the elevator. It opens. I go inside. It closes.

"What happened?" I ask. I hear a long sigh.

"You had to give half of your wealth to keep your friend alive," Lucifer's Champion says.

"I gave ten percent! And the other 40% is going to come from me buying stuff, which will—I don't know—like the money I spend will become someone else's money?"

"You got your friend killed, and you lost money. How is that possible."

I can tell he is trying to rattle me, but I don't let him. You gotta shake things like this off. Also, I bet that 10% is refundable. I press '7'. Button becomes red, and the word "GLUTTONY" appears.

Thirty-Six

I'm at Sammo's place, sitting on his futon. Sammo's got this little studio apartment in Burbank, California. Real shithole. We always fuck with him. "Hey Sammo, maybe in your next life you can be Jackie Chan!" We laugh, he doesn't, but that's how it goes.

Sammo and Frank Thomas are sitting on the couch. Their eyes are slightly farther apart, and all their face wrinkles are smoothed out. On the chair next to him is this black—God, I want to say "void"?— that sounds similar to Scary Mask. I know because the void is begging for money. An ERROR screen flashes in the middle of the studio apartment, and the black void disappears.

Everyone is taking Kahlua shots and laughing. Well, I'm not. I've got a glass of water. But we're all having a good time, I guess.

"Hey guys," Frank Thomas brings us to a hush. He's got this big, beautiful smile.

"I forgot to tell you where we are going tonight." We all look at each other wide-eyed. Not out of anticipation, but because normally I am the alpha male and make the decisions for the group. Frank is overstepping roles and responsibilities, so this better be good.

"Remember that club you enter from inside the visitors' locker room at Dodger Stadium? The one that Meryl Streep used to strip at?"

The room is now silent.

"Well, when Magic Johnson bought the Dodgers, he reopened it. And I got four—ERROR—three tickets for tonight."

Sammo can't believe it. Neither can I. This club has made and mostly broke every Hollywood star in the world. And with Magic at the reins? Holy shit. I hope to beat this Hell floor I have to fucking die because that is the most likely outcome.

"When can we head over?" I ask. Frank looks at me. His smile pulls up his face a little higher. His eyes go red.

"Whenever you want, Greg Maxwell—" Frank says.

"—You're the DD tonight." He and Sammo levitate off the couch and glide towards the door.

No.

No fucking way.

Never.

This can't be. The one chance I'll ever see anything that resembles this place, I'm going as some straight-edge DD jerkoff? What am I supposed to do all night? Walk around and do magic tricks or something? I'm not doing any magic. Not even sexy Criss Angel stuff. Fuck this shit.

I go to my classic get out-of-DD move: I pull my pants down and pull my butthole out and over the Kahlua bottle. Then, I run to the wall and do a guided headstand. The Kahlua bottle pours down into my rectum. A perfect buttchug. In seconds, I should be so drunk that I will be driven to the hospital to get my stomach pumped before I DD for a second.

A few seconds go by. Nothing. I pop the bottle out of my cheeks and pour the remaining liquid out. Water. I run over to the liquor cabinet. I pull bottles off the rack and start downing them. Brown ones, black ones, green ones, whatever. They all come out the same: water. I'm getting reverse-Jesus'd.

I also realize that I accidently gave myself an enema with that Kahlua bottle. Knowing that this is not Sammo's actual studio apartment, I shit all over his couch. I've made a fool of myself.

I don't get much time to clean myself up or think about how much this night will suck because we are somehow already in the car. They are all in the back, and I am in the front. God, they are loud. The drive from Burbank to Dodger Stadium takes a couple hours. I'm trying to listen to a Joe Rogan podcast, but these knuckleheads won't stop laughing and making memories with one another. I want to laugh, but I can't unlock the part of my brain that usually finds this shit hilarious. Sammo is going into his classic bit where he pulls out his dick and pushes the head of his penis down inside the shaft skin and pretends he still has his umbilical cord. I find it disgusting and unprovoked. I hate myself for thinking that. Normally, I am busting up. Also, listening to this Joe Rogan podcast fully sober is making me want to flip the car and kill all of us.

We get to Dodgers Stadium. I get these stumbling assholes up to the ticket counter. Frank Thomas can't remember the secret code. He suggests we just buy a ticket to the game and he'll get on the jumbo-tron, and Magic Johnson will see him and invite us down to party.

No dice. I've seen enough baseball.

I sober Frank Thomas up very quickly. How? Fine. You take a t-shirt covered in water, and you put it over the nose and mouth of a drunk person. Then you pour water on the t-shirt and in a couple minutes they are sober as a judge. Yeah, it's waterboarding, but I have shit to do. I calm Frank Thomas down. That takes a while because he was waterboarded. I think this is an interesting cultural thing because when I've waterboarded Sammo in the past, he gets it. Personally, I've never been waterboarded.

Turns out, there is no passcode. You just tell the ticket counter that you want to go to Magic Johnson's nightclub. So we do that. We get told to wait for our personal usher. So we wait.

Guess who our personal usher is? The guy from the JFK museum. Still a weirdo, but it's good to see real people. Apparently, he got fired because he was serving open drinks in his little JFK sex video grotto and they didn't have a liquor license. Yikes. He's like, "Yeah, the move across the country was tough," and I was like, "Do you like LA?" and he's like, "I'm not in LA, I'm in the Bleeding Tower."He says some other stuff, but I kind of tune him out until we get to the visitors' locker room.

The visitors' locker room is dull. Empty. There are chairs and lockers. Not much painting needed for this picture. We walk to the second-to-last locker. The museum guy kicks the back wall in, and now we can hear club music. Everyone is excited. Me? I dunno. It seems loud. Ugh. Is this the new me? I hate myself.

We go down a regular flight of stairs. Every bass note seems to get The Boys more excited. I can hear inside jokes they formed throughout this night. I don't understand any of them. If I had just one drink, I could be a little closer to them. Like a beer and a shot. I could loosen up, you know?

When we reach the last step of the staircase, the doors to the club open. It is everything. People are either fucking, crying, or attempting to kill themselves from being over-stimulated. All the drinks smell strong. There is a heavy bass vibrating everyone's butt cheeks. Greg Kinnear is doing a full-nude show in the birdcage hanging above the dance floor. I can tell everyone is either wet or rock solid. Except me. I'm in Hell.

My brain can't get on the same level as The Boys. Two seconds in, they are already knuckle-deep in this place. They got drinks, they got guns, women are begging them to have public sex. I have my phone. I have a glass of club soda that the bartender labeled as "NOT

ALCOHOL" so I can't fool anyone. This place stinks like buttholes and pubic hair sweat.

I try to order the tiniest bit of alcohol. One Zima. They won't let me.

"You're the DD, big guy. Just enjoy yourself," the bartender says.

I can't. I try everything. I try doing magic. I try networking. I tell a group of strangers I am planning a solo camping trip. No one wants to listen to me. I am the sober guy.

I look out on the dance floor. Sammo and Frank Thomas are babe'd and blacked out. They are holding each other at the waist while multiple women give them back massages. I am hurt. I am jealous. The club soda hurts my nose when I drink it too fast.

I jog out on the dance floor. I can't take it! Maybe we can all bond over the international language of dance. I do a quick child's pose to loosen up my hips. I pop back up, but I am hit with a wave of panic.

I can't remember any of my choreography. I embarrass everyone. Greg Kinnear stops dancing. The bass stops, and my cheeks tingle.

I am lifted off my feet by some of the dancers. They pass me from one person to another until I am off the dance floor. I am heartbroken. I walk over to the doors we came in. I wait for my friends so we can leave.

Are they even my friends? I hate these thoughts. I would see people post stuff like this online, and it sounded so dumb. But now those thoughts are in my head, and I feel dumb. I feel sad and alone, and it's because I can't drink or do drugs with The Boys. I keep trying to remind myself that this is only temporary and I gotta be strong, but I can't.

"You know," Derek says behind me. "There's a room here for people like you. You know, straight-edge people that can't really connect with their friends that still party cool and big time."

"Yeah?" I say.

"Yeah," Derek says. He extends his hand the way Doug used to. But this time it feels nice. I take his hand. He leads me through the crowded drunk people, away from my friends, to a small red door in the back.

Derek opens the door. The room is the size of a walk-in closet. There is a loaded gun sitting on an IKEA table.

"Greg, you know that life is pretty pointless now." He rubs my shoulders. "All of your friends forgot you when they took all those shots without you. And think about it, Greg,"

He turns me towards him. He gets his eyes looking right into mine.

"How easy would it have been for them to call a Lyft so you can drink with them?" Fucking great and devastating point. We are constantly using Lyft. Why now have DDs? When we have this opportunity? You party-cuck me now?

I walk over to the gun. Six-shooter. I spin the little round thing that holds the bullets. It makes the clicky noise I thought it would. I hold it up to my head. My finger is on the trigger. I am a couple millimeters away from a dirt nap, and I feel nothing. I look at Derek. I thought maybe he would be conflicted at watching me kill myself, but he is very aroused.

Ok. It looks like this is curtains for me.

Who knows, maybe there will be a Universe 40 where I can have friends who don't abandon me.

Like a speck of light, a super healthy thought pops into my head:

This is everybody else's fault. Not yours.

This thought feels good and true. Derek is whispering at me to pull the trigger. I still kind of want to, but I'm hesitant.

You deserve to party. No one else should get to determine how and when you party.

Derek is shaking.

You don't need to drink to have fun. You have a loaded gun. Who's going to tell you that you can't have fun?

Bingo.

I shoot Derek. Blam-o. Wait. Shit. I forgot that Derek was real. Not sure if that is murder. Probably is. Let the mathematicians and scientists of the world figure that out. I'm here for fun.

I storm out of the suicide room and make my way back to the dance floor where I started. Where I belong. I can tell by the looks I am getting that I am not wanted back. Well, too bad. Because I have a gun now.

I still can't find the beat. That makes me sad for a second. But why should I find the beat? I point the gun at the DJ. I think the beat should find me.

The DJ does some fiddling, and wouldn't you know it, I am dancing in perfect rhythm. I get everyone to form a circle around me to watch me dance. My friends are in the circle clapping. I made sure of it with my gun. Now I'm having a blast. I love dancing.

I get thirsty. Maybe it's time for me to get a drink. I order some shots for myself. Bartender still says no. Says it's part of this Hell floor and I can't have any alcohol. It's out of his control. He begs for me not to kill him. I don't.

But, I don't think it's fair that I can't drink and everyone else can. I have a gun. Shouldn't I be treated equally—or better—than the people around me? I make an executive decision. No one can drink.

Now that no one can drink and everyone has to do what I want, this place is starting to get pretty freaking cool. My friends suddenly want to talk to me and keep me happy. All these girls are giving me looks that I am choosing to interpret as sexy looks. Greg Kinnear's shift ended hours ago, but I like watching Greg Kinnear dance. So I ask Greg to stay. I point the gun at him. Not only does Greg want to stay, he practically begs me!

When it's time to leave, I don't really feel like driving my friends back home. Someone else should drive. I am able to find someone pretty quickly. Sammo, Frank Thomas, and I go over all the inside jokes they made while I was gone. We manage to integrate me into all those inside jokes. They are our inside jokes now.

Traffic is pretty heavy, but it manages to clear up when I hang my gun out the window. We are home in no time. I crash in Sammo's bed. Frank and Sammo sleep on the couch. We all decided that it was best. With my hand on the gun, I fall asleep.

Thirty-Seven

I wake up inside the elevator. I know better than to gloat, but, Jesus. I just dunked on this asshole.

"You know, I did come pretty close to killing myself," I tell him. I honestly feel kind of bad, so I am busting his balls but also consoling him. It must be hard designing all these floors. But you can't just let a guy have a gun and give nobody else a gun. What's the matter with you?

He says something like, "I'm 38-0. I'm undefeated. Fuck you," and I'm like, "Bro, I don't even remember the first 38 times." Then he's like, "Well, why don't you pick up the pace?" and I'm like, "I fucking will, give me these next two floors, let's FUCKING GO." I'm so jacked up at this point, I punch the wall to show him that when I punch, I punch hard. Message sent.

I press '8'. The button says "LUST". I can't even feel the rumble. The door opens. No scene change. No nothing. I charge out of the elevator like a fucking bull. I'm in a room. Door on the other end. Forty sets of titties. Eighty in total. The titties are perfect.

I want to touch the titties. Clearly, the room wants me to touch the titties. But jokes on the room: I'm actually enraged right now. I want to kill that asshole. He forced me to kill one of my friends. He almost made me hate my two main friends. I almost blew my brains out. I didn't get to perform with my new improv team. I'm done.

I'm also rock solid, penis-wise. Despite being so angry, I still have a reptile brain. I'm a sick monster. I have dark, primal needs.

But I can press forward. If this were the first room, I would have been done. Boom. Faceplant into a titty and probably, what, get my head blown off? But I've really been forced to do some self-exploration in this tower, and I'm starting to see that I haven't put the correct amount of value into my friendships and the more intellectual sides of my relationships.

I say all this with an erection that has taken all the blood from my legs. I can't walk. This gets me even more mad. This fucking guy has no idea who he is messing with. I mean, he probably knows more than anyone, ever, but Goddamnit, I'm so mad!

I scream like a full-blown animal. I scream so hard that I shoot a rope of rage cum. It shoots across the hallway. I manage to lift my right leg and walk it forward. Then my left. I slowly push forward.

This is real dog shit. I get to where my rage cum is pooling up on the ground and, you guessed it, I slip and break my ankle. Bone out. I throw up all over my hands. They will be sticky now. Great. I use all the liquid on the ground to penguin slide to the door. That goes well until I look up and see a pair of titties again.

Guess who is so rock solid they punched a hole into the ground? Uh, me. I can actually look through the boner hole I made and see Magic Johnson's nightclub from the floor below.

I can't keep doing the penguin slide because my boner is so skinny and sharp it keeps slicing through the wood and creates too much friction. It's at this moment I have a real, mentalist flashback moment: the boats on the cape. Sail boats!

I take my shirt off. I let off a quick rope of Me-Chowder over my head to pad the last 50 or so feet. I look at some titties, to get myself back to being rock solid. This ship is going to need a strong masthead.

I tie the shirt around my hog and fashion a sail of sorts. Then, I wait for wind to roll off the titties I have passed. Sure enough, my shirt sail billows, and I am off! At one point, I actually have to bring the sails down because I'm sliding too fast!

I fly past the exit door so fast that I don't get to take one more peek at the titties.

I end up back in the elevator. No shit. I immediately pop off, "Ahoy dipshit!" I stand up and check myself out. Perfectly dry, totally good to go.

"You know, you built this place wrong," I say. "Should have never let me have time for self-discovery. You fucked up."

"I fucked up?" Lucifer's Champion says.

"Yeah. You did."

"Oh did I?" He goes off camera. I hear him press a button. My ankle re-breaks. My shirt is drenched in cum. My hands are sticky.

"No, YOU fucked up. You should have watched your mouth," Lucifer's Champion tells me. We are fully escalated with each other. We get to the point where I got my hands on the TV, and I'm begging him to come into this elevator so I can get to the main course of ass kicking. Secretly, I love it. Just two alphas locking horns. Nothing cooler to see.

"You want to skip the last floor?" he says.

I'm like, "I didn't want to do any of these fucking floors. I wanted to fight you. You never said there were going to be nine goddamn floors."

"Fine, we can skip the last floor." Oh, shit. Didn't think that was a possibility. I ask what the last floor is.

"Why do you need to know what the last floor is, if you want to kick my ass right now?"

I hate how fair this question is. I want to know for a couple of reasons. One, I did eight floors (one omitted for religious purposes), so I'd like to finish up strong. Two, and this feels like the main one, is I might be dying soon and these potentially are my last moments alive. But I can't say that to Lucifer's Champion, for obvious reasons.

"Maybe I want to go in there because I heard this floor is where I date your mom and you become my stepson."

"Well, I don't know where you heard that. But that's a lie. It's a Chipotle."

Oh my god. I love Chipotle. But I play it cool.

"Is that where me and your mom meet for her lunchbreak because your mom works at Chipotle?"

"No."

"Do I take your mom to Chipotle for our first date?"

"No, and you don't even get to eat at Chipotle because everybody in front of you is a mom, each ordering for an entire soccer team. And all of them have never been to Chipotle."

I don't show it, but that floor seems brutal. I keep this close to the chest, but I would not have passed that one. Too many variables out of my control. A truly perfect floor to torment me.

"I will skip that floor. I'd like to come straight to you. And fight."

"I will allow it."

I press 'R'. No red light, no extra words. Not needed.

Thirty-Eight

I can feel my heart beating super fast. This is it. Big time. I'm gonna fight a no-shit demon. I locate my Cutco knives. When the doors open to the rooftop, I make a point to look for a bird or see some trees or listen to my breath because I feel like I need to have a moment or something. But, I dunno. I see a bird. I breathe a little. I gain nothing. Now I'm just standing on a roof with a bag of knives.

Lucifer's Champion is staring at the strip mall parking lot. I can see his dick from behind. He's got a real good back definition. Lot of lat stuff.

He turns to me. He must be, conservatively, nine feet tall. When he was on a cloud, he looked so much smaller. Jesus. Why did I rush up here?

In one hand, he is holding a glass of wine. His other hand is holding a sword.

"I hope you brought something for our battle, Greg Maxwell."

I show him the bag. He looks confused. I tell him the bag is filled with knives. That probably makes more sense. I kind of want to use the bag to hyperventilate. The only time I ever successfully fought a guy this size is when I slapped this Samoan guy twice in the face after he stole my clothes at a day spa. And in that case, I only got two slaps in because he was currently having a heart attack. EMTs told me to stop slapping him.

It was really sad—guy was at the spa for his 20th wedding anniversary—but I still count it as a fight I won.

Me and Lucifer's Champion are staring at each other. We're starting to look dumb.

"So, do we fight, or—?" I don't know how to kick this party off. I am blacked out during most fights.

Lucifer's champion smiles.

"Greg, you don't want to enjoy Earth one last time?"

"I did, I saw a bird. Unless you think I should see another bird, let's start fighting."

"Greg, I've seen you scale this tower 38 times. Every challenge encountered, defeated. Except me. What is it, Greg, that prevents you from beating me?"

"You're like, nine feet tall. Also, again, I don't remember the other 38 times, so why are you even bringing it up? I'm so sick of stupid people. Put your wine down, and let's do this."

"Actually, Greg, if you don't mind, I'd like to show you the other 38 times."

I don't even get a chance to say "I'd like to not see that" before he does his own little IMAX thing. He doesn't have the styling or presentation of Doug. Doug really brought it. Xandra, too. I gotta say, after going through the floors and seeing this IMAX thing, I feel comfortable saying that Lucifer's Champion lacks attention to detail. The guy forgot faces. He didn't research The Road to Hana. Overall, bad.

Whatever, I watch his little thing. Production value is bad. It is your poorest friend's Bar Mitzvah montage. There's a Comic Sans title:

Greg and LC's Battles

Lee Ann Womack's "I Hope You Dance" starts playing. Slow montage of every universe version of me. I look different in every universe. Some I look like absolute shit. Some I look fantastic. Some I am blue. Some I have no arms. There is one where I am entirely a pool of silver liquid.

The fighting begins. The music is still playing. Jesus, these fights are quick:

- Universe 1: LC grabs the back of my head, rams it through his sword. Dead within seconds.

- Universe 2: I clearly know martial arts. I do a few flashy kicks and peacock a little. LC twists my head off. I manage to get one headless kick off.

- Universe 3: I try to headbutt him. Can't reach his head, my face gets buried in his dick and balls. I suffocate and die.

- Universe 4: Hey, I throw a ninja star! Right out of the gate. Hits him right in the chest. Bounces off. LC is mad. He charges me. I try to apologize. He kicks my head in. I die.

- Universe 5: I'm trying to make a bunch of portals to jump through. Fairly decent idea. I'm not doing any damage, but I'm not dead. Oh, oops: looks like LC figured out he can go through the portals too. That clearly surprises me because I'm now crying. LC catches up to me. Nasty tearing sounds. My limbs are getting thrown out of every different portal I made. Clearly dead.

- Universe 6: Wow. I actually try to kill myself. LC stops me. We talk about it?? Then he tears me in half.

- Universe 7: Did not make it to the roof—got stuck on floor two.

- Universe 8: I pretend to not be me? I pretend to be LC's cousin? And I'm visiting for the weekend. What? LC doesn't buy it (buddy, he saw you come out of the elevator in your disguise). Body slams me into the ground. Of course, I die.

- Universe 9: I have a series of powders. I'm, like, a sorcerer type. The fucking wind BLOWS my powders away. Now I'm just a guy in a fancy silk robe. LC gives me a bear hug and breaks my entire body. Dead. Takes the silk robe. Puts it on. Doesn't fit. Throws it off the edge.

- Universe 10: Did not make it to the roof—got stuck on floor six.

- Universe 11: Okay. This time, it looks like I brought a bomb. Bunch of wires. I throw it in his direction. I laugh because he only has one minute to diffuse the bomb. He diffuses the bomb in fourteen seconds. He drags me by my hair towards the bomb. He makes me eat the bomb. I eat the entire bomb. I can't move because I'm too full. I lay in the fetal position for eight hours. I eventually have to shit out the bomb. I die from shitting out my own bomb.

- Universe 12: This is when he starts doing a montage before we fight. I try to fight him during the montage. He kills me fast enough that my death actually got thrown into the montage at the end.

- Universe 13: Did not make it to the roof—got stuck on floor four.

- Universe 14: I brought a gun. Gun goes off in my bag. Bullet hits my leg. I bleed out in the middle of the montage. Dead.

- Universe 15: Oh, martial arts is back! Goes just as bad.

- Universe 16: LC charges at me. I try to charge back at him. I try to run up his body and flip kick his chin. Needless to say, I do not do that. I trip before I reach him. My bottom half hits the ground. My top half is still falling when he grabs me by the shoulders and snaps me over myself like a lawn chair. Eventually, I die.

- Universe 17: He turns me into a sock puppet. Figure that one out yourself.

- Universe 18: Did not make it to the roof—got stuck on floor nine.

- Universe 19: I can fly in this universe. I know this because I say, "Let's take this fight to the AIR." I can tell flying was a big part of my personality. But LC doesn't want to take this fight to the air. He throws his sword clear through my stomach. Unable to fly. Dead.

- Universe 20: Oh, this is when I am a silver puddle. I do puddle stuff. LC scoops me into a bucket. Throws me over the side of the tower. Splat. I hear myself scream. Dead.

- Universe 21: LC throws the ninja star at me that I threw at him back in Universe 4. Does not bounce off me. Goes clean into my skull. Hits all the brain parts it needs to. I die.

- Universe 22: In this universe, I am taller than him by a solid forty feet. Doesn't matter. I have no arms. My legs have no bend. I'm basically a really big cucumber. Based on sheer size, this one takes a while, but it's not even close. He punches me so many times that my skin gives way and he's able to dissect me with his fingers. Dead.

- Universe 23: Did not make it to the roof—got stuck on floor five.

- Universe 24: LC looks bored. He doesn't even fight me. He kind of lays my body down and jumps on my back after getting a running start. Oh, wait. He is trying to skim board. I am still very much alive during the first ten attempts. Once my body breaks up and blood pours out, there is enough lubrication to get some sliding going. After attempt twenty, he is skimming pretty well, and I am dead. He seems recharged. Really nice energy about him.

  "I Hope You Dance" ends. Two seconds later, it starts up again.

- Universe 25: Wow. I bring out some scalding hot chain links. This is going to go poorly. And it does. LC takes the chains and fashions a noose. Guess where my head goes? Right in that noose. He chokes me so hard the hot chains go clean through my neck and my head falls off. No blood because the skin burned over.

- Universe 26: I mean, I die (duh), but LC is wearing a shirt. And pants.

- Universe 27: I die again, but LC's pants and shirt are gone. He tried something, it didn't work, and he was big enough to admit it.

- Universe 28: Did not make it to the roof—got stuck on floor seven.

- Universe 29: I'm not a puddle, but LC still puts me in a bucket and throws me over the side of the tower. Big splat. Clearly dead.

- Universe 30: Did not make it to the roof—got stuck on floor one.

- Universe 31: LC must have had plans, because this time he was standing right outside the elevator. When the elevator door opens, he screams, "COMBAT BEGINS NOW!" and stabs me very quickly. I die.

- Universe 32: Did not make it to the roof—got stuck on floor eight.

- Universe 33: Rips my arms clean off. I'm screaming and crying. LC comes up and tries to hand me my arms. I go to reach for them, but I don't have arms to reach for my arms. Fuck. LC is no-shit hilarious. I die.

- Universe 34: LC tries to make our combat a riddle-based thing, but he keeps telling the riddle wrong. I'm mouthing off, telling him he's not a riddle guy. He gets flustered and gives up the riddle thing. Cuts my head off. I'm dead, but nobody really won.

- Universe 35: Did not make it to the roof—got stuck on floor three.

- Universe 36: I say, "Bones OUT," but instead of his bones flying out of his body, my bones fly out of my body. Super frustrating. I'm dead.

- Universe 37: Make it to the rooftop, but I refuse to come out of the elevator. Starve to death. Really embarrassing.

- Universe 38: I have a katana. Folded Japanese steel. Our swords clash. My sword shatters. I'm trying to put the pieces together. He offers to help. He picks up some. I pick up some. I put my pieces in one pile. He puts his pieces inside the back of my head. I basically died from teamwork and cleanliness.

The video ends with a title screen:

We are so proud of you, Jacob
Mazel Tov

"I keep forgetting to take that out," Lucifer's Champion says. The whole thing disappears.

Overall, not good. Lucifer's Champion has some serious range. He clearly has never seen Cutco knives, so I feel like I'm still the favorite. But Jesus. I wish I had that fucking Beam Capsule.

"Okay, let's do thirty seconds of personal preparation, and then after that, I guess we just get after it. Sound good?"

Lucifer's Champion nods. He throws his wine off the tower. He grips the sword in his two meaty hands. I start fumbling through my bag to take stock of what I have.

Five steak knives
One grater
One pair of scissors
A serrated knife
One, like, smaller steak knife?
A big, triangle-shaped knife
A big, curvy knife

154

A bag of cocaine (very cool)

I very quickly do the cocaine. *Now it's a party,* I say to myself, out loud, in screaming form. What I can respect is that he has not rushed me this whole time. For that, I bow to him, but I kind of abort the bow halfway through because this guy has done a lot more bad than good. I hold all the cutlery in my two hands.

We reach the thirty second mark.

He charges. God, holy shit, he is fast. He gets a pretty good, if not great, punch to my face, neck, and chest. All with one fist. Hands are huge. His fist is like a harder version of a footrest. I am so rattled that, as he gallops by, I accidentally stab myself in the leg. I am able to pry out the blade using the scissors. I look up, and he is laughing and pouring himself some more wine. So far, it feels like a draw.

"Greg Maxwell! Are you weary from your journey? Do you have nothing left for me?"

I don't answer this question because it is patronizing. Also, if I say that I *do* have more left, I'm kind of taking 'Draw' off the table. At this point, I'd settle for a draw. He can rule, like, the Midwest, and we'd be even.

"Don't worry Greg, I will not kill you right away. This is the last time we will meet. I would like to take my time."

He charges again. This time, I can tell he wants to use the sword. I grab the cheese grater with one plan in mind. It's gonna be some real kamikaze shit, but I'm running low on non-kamikaze ideas. When he swings the sword, I duck. Unfortunately, he chose to do a vertical slash, and that sword comes right down on my buttcrack, and now my ass crack goes six more inches up my spine. Lot of blood.

But as he is going by me, my grater rakes his chest. He screams in pain. When he gallops away, I look down at my grater. Got it. One demon nipple. Came clean off.

"I'M BACK IN THE GAME, MOTHERFUCKER."

He looks confused.

"You struck your first blow in our history. Well done. But do you think my nipple equals your gaping wound?"

"Big difference, asshole: you can't eat my gaping wound." I eat his nipple. Welcome to Earth, bitch. You want to fight? Be prepared for parts of your body to get eaten.

This sets him off. He gallops at me again. So far, I am doing pretty bad at blocking any of his stuff. I don't have any plan, and he is getting extremely close. He raises his sword. I hold my buttcheeks together so I don't shit myself when he kills me.

I close my eyes. I hear a thump. I hear hooves slip on the concrete. I hear the sound of plastic, grinding, cocking, firing. I open my eyes. I follow the stream of darts back to a ledge on the side of the roof.

A young man in tattered boys' clothes is holding a Nerf gun. He looks grizzled. Mean. A real dude.

"Ethan!"

"Greg." This doesn't sound like the Ethan who needed me to cut his birthday cake for him.

"You're like a no-shit Mad Max guy!"

"Now is not the time. I can distract him for a bit. It's time to make your move."

Lucifer's Champion gets back on his hooves. Ethan hits him with another dart. I grab steak knives and start to do my business. I get a running start at Lucifer's Champion. I slide under Lucifer's Champion while stabbing his stomach. His big thick abs are bending the knives, but I see blood. His dick keeps slapping me in the face, but it's totally fine. Before Lucifer's Champion can grab me, Ethan hits him with a Nerf dart. And I can tell they hurt more than he thought they would hurt. That stupid fucking gun is finally paying dividends.

We get a couple rounds of that going. I'm able to get a real good stomach wound on him. But this guy is a fucking bull.

We run out of darts. So it becomes this whole thing where Ethan and I are trying to run around and grab these foam darts and load them into his gun while Lucifer's Champion slaps us around. By that, I mean he is violently stabbing us. By the time we get the darts in the gun, I am, like, pretty much dead. Ethan can't even hold the gun because he has no more hands. Jesus. Why did you even come, Ethan?

Lucifer's Champion clearly wants one more charge at me. And he's gonna get it. I got nothing left. I go, like, distant-vision-misty-eyed-gladiator style where I'm staring in the distance. But this asshole is so huge, he is the foreground and the distance. I focus on the little wound I made in his stomach. Nobody can say I came up here and did nothing. I took a pretty good chunk out of Lucifer's finest. Not bad for a blue-collar Major League Baseball general manager.

I study the shape. Maybe it's my misty Russell-Crowe-Gladiator eyes, but that flesh wound kind of looks like Xandra's vagina.

I feel a blood pouch form. Thick, in my pubic bone, but also in my taint area. Just to amuse myself—I am bored at this point—I start to push the blood up into my penis. I think about Xandra. But not just her body. Her personality. Her soul. I think about my friends and this earth and how we can hurt each other, but we have endless opportunities to heal one another, and I get so fucking thick, all of my flesh wounds stop bleeding so I can have enough blood to keep my hog staying strong. I am feeling some no-shit love.

I hold my arms wide. When Lucifer's Champion attempts to strike, I embrace. He screams.

His chest against mine, my hog through his stomach and out his back, I feel all the love of the last universe I was born to protect. I start to suck on his remaining nipple, running my free thumb against the patch where his other nipple used to be. I can feel his hog getting thick under me. He cries because he knows his erection plays right into my hand. With each pump of blood, his hog raises me higher, pulling my hog further up his chest cavity. My hog, thin, grows sharper with each scream. I keep sucking until my face is equal with his.

"Looks like thirty-nine's the charm, huh, fuckface?" I say to him, romantically.

Then I open-mouth kiss him as my hog slices through his neck and cuts right down the middle of his brain. I do a shitty backflip off his hog as his body splits in half. I land on my shoulder, which hurts really bad. While I am on the ground, I see the sky clear as demons fall from the sky. A bird chirps. Whatever.

"Greg..." I hear Ethan moan. We both shuffle to our feet. He starts trying to look through his little book bag with his little stumps. He manages to pull out a black polo shirt. On the chest, a Souplantation logo.

"Xandra," I say. Ethan nods.

"I met her in a Lyft line. She said she was coming from dropping you off at the Bleeding Tower. She...spoke to you."

"During the Padres game." I start to tell Ethan about how I had sex with her for 15 years and another time, when I almost couldn't get an erection, but he shakes his head.

"She's in a coma. It was too much for her. Speaking through the tower floor. I'm sorry." He hangs his head. I say something like, "I'm sure she'll be fine," and then I shrug. I honestly forgot what Ethan just said. I put my arm around him. We look out at a world we will have to rebuild.

"Ethan, what I just did back there might have been rape. It was definitely murder. But you saw that he was going to murder me, right?"

"Of course."

"So, it's settled: I had to rape him."

"You had to kill him."

"Right. That's what I said."

And in that moment, we're just two regular guys shooting the shit on a rooftop.

Thirty-Nine

In the distance, I see two beautiful eagles making their way towards the rooftop Ethan and I are standing on. In the talons of each eagle are two men screaming their heads off. Behind the eagles, the sky is clearing up and becoming a normal blue. All the winged creatures are landing on the ground or on parked cars. Giant mess. Tons of damage.

But I'm more focused on the screams. I know those screams. The Boys! Frank and Sammo. No Scary Mask. He really did die, huh. My memory is pretty sharp, and I remember not having a clear-cut way to prevent that.

The eagles are far enough away that I can safely turn to Ethan and tell him I am proud of the man he has become. He says that he has a lot of things from his childhood that he will finally be able to process and that he hopes I will make myself available, but I dunno. You don't just throw that on people.

The eagles are getting a lot closer now, so I tell him that he should start making his way down the tower and once I get some general housekeeping stuff done, I'll send him an email or something. He says he doesn't have hands so getting down the tower will be tough. Lots of things are tough. He mumbles something about me and my personality. If he has to mumble it, it must have not been worth hearing. Ethan leaves, somehow.

KEITH JAMES

The eagles land on the roof. They are super ginger with The Boys. They drop them on top of the tower next to me and fly away. "Getting down from this tower is going to be a bitch," I say to The Boys.

They are fucking gobsmacked by the sharpness of my erection. "Can we touch it," Sammo begs. "Not unless you want to end up like that guy," I say. We all laugh.

Frank pulls me aside. "You don't need to say you wrote screenplays or beat Tony Hawk in SKATE anymore. You saved Earth."

I hold his midsection with both of my hands. "I don't *need* to do those things because I *did* do those things. And on top of that, I saved *Earth*." I give him a bro'd-out kiss on the lips. He gives me a 70% kiss back. I choose to not read into that. Friendship repaired.

"Hey, I heard Trader Ed's is staying open late tonight. If we catch a plane, we could be on the dance floor in five hours," Sammo says.

"Why are they keeping it open?"

"You, goof!" Sammo pulls on my fingers.

While me and The Boys are high-fiving and deciding what drinks we are going to get first, I can't pull myself away from all the dead bodies spread out across Rancho Bernardo. I bet Nebraska looks like shit. I think about Xandra lying in a hospital bed like a fucking carrot stick. And I am gonna go dance and fuck and drink all night and make super great memories?

I don't know. I pull away from the high-fives and turn my back towards The Boys. That's all I needed. Some fresh air away from the musk of those two kings.

I give it some thought inside my cushion of fresh air. Man, it's so obvious what we have to do.

"Boys, we don't party on the Cape tonight." They look at me like I'm fucking dumb.

"But we will party."

161

I use my katana-sword-like dick to jam into the side of the bleeding tower. I put Sammo and Frank on my back, and we slide down the side of the tower as my dick meat slows down our descent. I use the time we are sliding down to explain our mission, including roles and responsibilities for the crew.

Once we hit the ground, we are in full party-mob mode. I'm behind the wheel of a hotwired car. Sammo is getting out to rob liquor stores. Frank is dialing up every man, woman, rabbit, and other friendly animal and making sure they all know how to get to hospital room 2185 at Sharp Memorial. Why room 2185? That's Xandra's room. Even though she is fully coma'd, she came in clutch. And because she came in clutch, she is in a coma. Full circle. She needs to party.

We get to room 2185 and clear out some space for a solid dance floor and a rollie cocktail bar. I'm going back and forth with the nurses trying to figure out what is essential to Xandra's survival and what isn't. They say it's all important, and I'm like, "I get it: we're negotiating. But I got, like, 60 people rolling in, so let's just get to an agreement fast."

We settle on getting rid of the bed. She's in a coma. She's getting great sleep. Kids get great sleep in sleeping bags. I dunno. We prop her up on a chair. She looks great. This party is for her, so I'm glad someone made her look nice. I ask the nurses if this is in poor taste. Their answer is different than my answer.

People and animals start rolling in, and we are fucking out of our heads. We saved Earth! I saved Earth, but when you are partying with people, 'I's' become 'We's,' and that's fine. We keep kicking cords out of Xandra but not on purpose. We're partying. And also, if we kick a cord out, we put it back. Calm down.

During one of the thousand slow songs, Rudy crawls up my leg and whispers into my ear.

"You deserve a vacation." I know. I do a lot for everyone. But I dunno. I keep seeing all those bodies outside, and I guess I'm, like, the unofficial king of Earth? I think there's a lot more shit I gotta do.

First thing I have to do is be sweet and caring to my comatose soulmate. She coma'd for me. For the world. I'm gonna have to do things like shave her little mustache and read her books. There's no room for my Tempur-Pedic, so I'll probably have to sleep in a chair. She may be in this coma all weekend, but I'll never leave her side.

"*This* is my vacation." I motion vaguely over to Xandra. Rudy doesn't know what that means and neither do I, but it seemed like a nice thing to say, so I said it.

Acknowledgements:

First, big thanks to Marty and Andy at Humorist Books. You took a chance, and backed a complete moron.

I wrote the first draft of this book three years ago. I asked everyone I knew on Facebook (perfectly normal and cool website) if they wanted to read the first draft of my book. A group of people not only said they wanted to read it, but actually read the book.

Lauren Flynn
Jason Casey
Ben Lieberman
Margaret Dilloway
Justin Pierson
Katie Kromelow
Courtney Hale
Matt Jent
Jesse Suphan

I've done art stuff for a majority of my life. It is lonely. There are times when I wasn't even looking for praise, but a simple, "I acknowledge your existence." To the people up top: you'll never know how much your simple act changed my life.

I want to give a special thanks to Hudson Reynolds. Hudson, you were a little freak for this book. A right pervert. Without your encouragement, this book would have not found the loving home it has at Humorist Books.

Thank you to everyone who virtually came out to the book reading, braved the rough waters of Eventbrite ticket limits and the crippling strength of Zoom passwords.

To the Sandrew family: every one of you opened your life to me in some way. Ryan, the godfather of my firstborn child: I've asked all our mutual friends if they think you have peaked, and not a single one said yes. I'm starting to believe them ☺. Jared, you've been reading my work for almost fifteen years. Your support has been constructive, patient, and has gotten me nowhere. I'll never forgive you. Linsey, hey girl! Have an outstanding summer. Barry, I was a piss poor Comic-Con employee in your eyes, yet you never struck me in anger. Such courage. Lori, I came to you in tears asking if I could live in your house. You said fine, then we sat on the couch, and you told me who from my theater program had gotten fat. Thank you.

Angela and Courtney, thank you for reading the book and for being part of the family I chose. I'd choose you two every time. JC, you have told me time and time again that you "don't read", and for that level of honesty, I choose you, too.

Last, my wife Marley, and my little Daisy. Marley, I wrote this book in five-thousand-word chunks. After I finished a chunk, I would print it out and hand it to you. You'd sit on the couch, and I would go into another room because I was too nervous. I would listen for your laughter. Hearing you laugh kept this thing alive. Making you laugh keeps me going. Thank you for everything you do, and everything you are. I love you.

Daisy, Daddy loves you very much. No one in this book is good, but you are. Our time together has just begun. Let's have fun!

About the Author

Keith James is a writer and performer from San Diego, California. He has trained and performed at Pack Theater, iO West, and UCB. His written work can be found in *McSweeney's*, Second City's *Points in Case*, the *Taco Bell Quarterly*, and others. He also writes and hosts the *Gus Biblowitz: Basketball Legend* audio series. One day, he will die.